Praise for *Isolated Incident*:

"Absorbing, earnest, and beautifully written, *Isolated Incident* is a loving por-
trayal of Canadians besieged by hate-crimes. Through fluid and insightful
storytelling Mariam Pirbhai shows how each must rise above grief, rage, and
despair to face the price and dangers of belonging."

—SHAUNA SINGH BALDWIN, author of *The Tiger Claw*,
What the Body Remembers and *English Lessons*

"Mariam Pirbhai is a consummate storyteller, deftly navigating the complexi-
ties of identity, family and faith during dangerous times. *Isolated Incident* is an
important novel portraying the often-neglected stories of a community under
siege but rarely given voice."

—CARRIANNE LEUNG, author of *That Time I Loved You*

"*Isolated Incident* will make all readers rethink what it means to be Canadian
today and what it might mean tomorrow were we to awaken to the realities
lived by the marginalized within Canadian borders. A must-read, urgent, and
topical."

—MYRIAM J A CHANCY, author of *What Storm, What Thunder*

"A thoughtful and intelligent examination of faith and intolerance centred
around a vicious attack on a Toronto mosque. Through the perspectives of
a rich cast of characters who are forced to navigate a landscape riddled with
hate crimes against Canadian Muslims, Pirbhai gives us a glimpse into the
complex reality of a community rarely depicted in the popular media."

—TASNEEM JAMAL, author of *Where the Air Is Sweet*

"Subverting . . . Orientalist scripts through which Muslims are too often rep-
resented, Mariam Pirbhai masterfully crafts authentic, real-life narratives of
Canadian Muslims trying to negotiate belonging in a land that has become
increasingly hostile to their faith and identity. A compelling story at a time
where Islamophobia has reached deadly proportions in Canada and around
the globe."

—DR JASMINE ZINE, author of *Under Siege:
Islamophobia and the 9/11 Generation*

"*Isolated Incident* is an absorbing tale that probes deeply into the links between migration and indigeneity, on the one hand, and misogyny and Islamophobia, on the other. This is just as much a story of place, land, and river as it is a story of love, violence, and belonging in the Americas. Faced with hate crimes, Mariam Pirbhai's characters struggle, question, and find peace in ways that will stay with readers long after turning the last page. We all need to read this outstanding novel with so much to teach about how to endure."

—Dr Shazia Rahman, author of *Place and Postcolonial Ecofeminism: Pakistani Women's Literary and Cinematic Fictions*

"Pirbhai's novel is an awakening to a new consciousness of articulation and performance of Muslimness. A compelling read!"

—Dr Aroosa Kanwal, co-editor of *The Routledge Companion to Pakistani Anglophone Writing*

ISOLATED INCIDENT

a novel

MARIAM PIRBHAI

In appreciation,

(Aug. '23)

MAWEN**Z**I
HOUSE

We acknowledge the support of the Canada Council for the Arts for our publishing program. We also acknowledge support from the Government of Ontario through the Ontario Arts Council, and the support of the Government of Canada through the Canada Book Fund.

Cover design by Mariam Pirbhai and Sabrina Pignataro
Author photo by Ronaldo Garcia

This is a work of fiction. Names, characters, events and incidents are the products of the author's imagination, or used in a fictitious manner.

Fahmida Riaz quote from "Mantra" in *Four Walls and a Black Veil*. Oxford University Press, 2004. Translated by Patricia L Sharpe.

E Pauline Johnson quote from *Flint and Feather: The Complete Poems of E Pauline Johnson (Tekahionwake)*. Hodder and Stoughton, 1972.

Song lyrics in Epilogue by James Gordon, "She is Fickle." Album: *The Song the River Sings*. Pipe Street Records, 2004.

Library and Archives Canada Cataloguing in Publication

Title: Isolated incident : a novel / Mariam Pirbhai.

Names: Pirbhai, Mariam, 1970- author.

Identifiers: Canadiana (print) 20220264767 | Canadiana (ebook) 20220264775 | ISBN 9781774150887
    (softcover) | ISBN 9781774150894 (EPUB) | ISBN 9781774150900 (PDF)

Classification: LCC PS8631.I73 I76 2022 | DDC C813/.6—dc23

Printed and bound in Canada by Coach House Printing

Mawenzi House Publishers Ltd.
39 Woburn Avenue (B)
Toronto, Ontario M5M 1K5
Canada

www.mawenzihouse.com

To my parents,
in loving memory

Magnificent River,
Hear the tale of my terrible fate,
My destiny was always in
A cruel hand. My kinship
With the land was snapped—like that!
A fearsome whirlwind, witch-like, red-eyed,
Swept me away and dropped me
In unfamiliar lands.

FAHMIDA RIAZ

And up on the hills against the sky,
A fir tree rocking its lullaby,
Swings, swings,
Its emerald wings,
Swelling the song that my paddle sings.

E PAULINE JOHNSON

Prologue

It wasn't much to look at. A store front in a strip mall. Were it not for those tortured words—masjid, jami, ibn-something or other—it was camouflaged by ordinariness, like deer antlers in a boreal forest. That was its treachery. Blending in and claiming to belong while it rejected everything you held sacred. Your rights. Your way of life. Your freedom. Building its arsenal of terror behind closed doors and nonsensical script. In books spewing blasphemy and lies. One God. Allah. The Prophet. He who will not be named. And peace shall not be upon Him. Not as long as there is light to guide the righteous. Not as long as there were more like himself. Soldiers. Soldiers, prepared to do what it takes, he thought, withdrawing a spray can, a baseball bat and a shopping bag from the trunk of his car.

He strode up to the building, setting his sights on the store sign, the door and the wall of brick and glass, striking hard against misguided talk of refuge and welcome with calculated swings, making his message stick in slow, steady streaks of red. He stopped to read the letter one last time, the one he'd taken pains to write in terms plainspoken and purposeful, and wrapped it carefully around the river rock he'd brought with him. From the shopping bag he withdrew the book he'd lifted from a local thrift store, and doused it with lighter fuel, setting it aflame. Taking aim, he pitched the burning Quran and the rock and letter into the godforsaken place those infidels always hid behind in plain sight.

He stepped back to look at his creation. We have been more than patient, he said to the shadow cast in shattered glass. We have been more than fair.

I

Writing on the Wall

1

Kashif Siddiqui knew he was in the right place. Ishaq-bhai had texted the mosque address to him and the other volunteers, but he hadn't said much else: *Trouble at Masjid Omar Bin Al-Hamad. All hands on deck.*

During his bus ride to Rexdale from North York, where he lived, there had been time to speculate: Was someone in trouble? Had there been a fallout? He imagined this was the kind of thing Ishaq-bhai, as the director of the Islamic Cultural Centre, might be called on to handle. Kashif hadn't, for a moment, entertained the idea that *trouble* meant something levelled *against* the mosque. Nor that trouble, in the plain-Jane strip malls of the Toronto suburbs, could look like this: like the site of a drone attack or an air strike.

"Hey, what took you so long!" someone called out. It was Nasser, standing beside a door leaning sideways from a broken hinge.

"What the heck!" Kashif rubbed the last remnant of sleep from his eyes.

Nasser, who was all spruced up in a business suit, thrust a broom into Kashif's hand before he could even ask about the gaping hole where the entrance to the prayer hall should have been, much less about the dented store sign, its Arabic script crossed out with fat red lines, or the chunks of brick and mortar strewn about like at a demolition site.

"The maulana's got a heart condition so they called on Ishaq-bhai to do the PR stuff—you know, the press, and all that," Nasser said.

"Sure," Kashif mumbled, distracted by the graffiti plastered across the building, even on the broken door. If you could call it graffiti. It was more like a scene out of a Halloween film, red paint dripping from a wall of words Kashif was only just starting to make out: *Death to Islam. Terrorist Scum. Go Back to Where You Came From. Our Home is NOT Your Home and Native Land . . .*

"There he is now." Nasser pointed to a goateed man touring the building with a white guy snapping photos, a camera bag slung over his shoulder.

"Who's the other guy?"

"Shit!" Nasser picked a piece of glass out of his shoe. "I don't know—the insurance agent or a reporter."

"Makes sense." Kashif said, finally able to take in the scene before him for what it was. For what it really was. A hate crime.

Kashif started sweeping up the glass but Nasser stopped him. "I should have mentioned that Ishaq-bhai asked us to hold off until all the pictures are taken."

"You could have opened with that!" Kashif muttered but acquiesced, leaning the broom against a wall.

"And there's the issue of the letter, too."

"What letter?" Kashif asked and felt a pat on his shoulder. He turned around to see Zafar, a friend who was another volunteer at the Islamic Cultural Centre.

"Threats, man. What else?"

"Did you read it?" Kashif started, but Nasser was already heading back to his car.

"I've got to get to work. I'll be back later."

Nasser's departure reminded Kashif that he had to take his mom to her doctor's appointment later that morning. Normally, his dad would have taken care of this kind of stuff but things had changed since he'd gone MIA. More like he'd been AWOL for the last year—he wasn't missing so much as he was just absent. Absent by choice. A deserter. And yet Kashif felt like a traitor for ignoring his calls. It wasn't as if he wanted to avoid his dad. He just hadn't worked out what he was supposed to say. What *could* he say to a man who'd turned his back on his wife when she was so ill? But after the last round of "Please call" texts or "It's your father" voicemails, things had gone silent. Like he'd given up. Kashif tried to convince himself it was for the best, but a day didn't go by when he didn't stare at "Hassan Siddiqui—aka Dad" in his Contact list. Not a day went by when he didn't *almost* hit "Reply" to one of those texts.

"Have the police been here yet?" Zafar asked.

"Not sure," Kashif came around.

"Who would do something like this!"

Kashif followed Zafar as he went about taking in the battered site.

"Tell me about it."

"Well, we can't just stand around, all shell-shocked."

"We probably should wait."

"God, where would we start, anyway!"

"I don't know about you," Kashif shielded his eyes from the sun rising in an orange blaze over the city, "but I'd start with that: with the writing on the wall."

2

A rubah Anwar opened the campus washroom faucet and released a slow trickle of water. She rolled up her sleeves, folding them carefully over her elbows, and dipped her hand into the running water. It was ice-cold. She washed her right hand three times, making sure the water reached between the fingers and up to the wrist. She repeated the process with her left hand, then leaned in closer to rinse her mouth and then her nose, careful to inhale and expel just enough to wash out any impurities, the water flowing through her nostrils like a neti pot.

Another young woman entered the washroom, went up to another sink and started to perform her ablutions, flinching from the cold water as Arubah had done minutes earlier. Arubah hiked up her jeans to expose her ankles, which she angled under the faucet. She recalled how difficult it was to perform this step in the regular washrooms, where she would have to hoist a foot over the sink and wash herself in that contorted position as people came in and out. She had been mortified on overhearing one of the janitors complain about having to mop up after "people like *them*." Now that the university had a specially designed and allocated washroom for Muslim students, she didn't feel so self-conscious. The stools were a really nice touch, she thought, though the faucet should have been placed lower, like the ones at the Islamic Cultural Centre, so the water didn't have to fall from such a height.

"Ashhadu an la ilaha illallahu. There is no God but Allah," Arubah recited in Arabic, completing her ablutions.

She gathered her things and stepped out into the hall, joining a stampede of students scrambling to make the ten minutes between classes count. She, too, would have to make a cross-campus dash to her Gender and Social Justice course right after juma, the weekly Friday prayer service. She always made an extra effort to get to Professor March's course early enough to save a seat for Marisol, her closest friend since sophomore year.

Arubah was grateful that she and Marisol were in so many of the same classes for their Women and Gender Studies major. She was doubtful their paths would have crossed otherwise. Marisol was born and raised in Montreal, daughter of a Guatemalan mother and Lebanese father, all of which gave her a touch of the exotic. And then there was a whole *other side* to her friend—the side Arubah preferred to keep at arm's length; the side that made things between them unnecessarily complicated. Arubah didn't think of herself as particularly complicated. She was a suburban Torontonian, born and raised north of the 401; she saw herself as Muslim Canadian first, the daughter of Pakistani immigrants, second; and, unlike Marisol who lived on residence and came to uni on her parents' dime, Arubah lived with her mom and paid for tuition with government loans and bursaries and, up until her senior year, a part-time job at a biscuit factory. But, as different as they appeared, Arubah couldn't imagine getting through uni without Marisol, and she hoped they would remain friends long after graduation.

Arubah propped her elbows on the desk in the pie-shaped auditorium that reminded her of a half-moon crescent.

"The horrific honour killings of two Canadian teens by their Muslim father has marked a turning point . . . " Professor March, a slender woman with an asymmetrical bob, paused to adjust the portable microphone attached to her jacket lapel, a shrill reverb filling the room.

Arubah flipped through the pages of the assigned reading. "Wasn't another woman also killed in that case?" she whispered to Marisol.

"Hunh?" Marisol grunted.

"An adult woman was also killed there—not just the girls." Arubah flipped through her notes, confirming her suspicions: the case they were studying involved the murder of the man's daughters and his first wife, yet Professor March had only referred to the two daughters. The man's second wife was his accomplice, and the prof hadn't mentioned her either.

"Sorry about that!" Professor March's voice piped through the sound system. "As I was saying, this gruesome case not only shocked the nation but also had considerable implications for the Canadian Charter of Rights and Freedoms, at least where the rather broad interpretation of religious beliefs and practices is concerned."

In the few minutes remaining, the professor looked up at the class and asked if there were any questions.

Arubah had so many questions, she found it hard to say something coherent. Professor March's omission of the female victim clearly slanted the case in a certain direction. And then she seemed to take the media's coverage of the case at face value, particularly the way they constantly referred to the man as Muslim, and referred to his daughters as Canadian. Weren't they all Canadians? And why was this guy, and not also his female accomplice, the prof's main focus? He was guilty as sin, of course, but so was she.

"Yes? The student in the third row from the back?" Professor March stepped away from the podium to field a question. Arubah wondered why all eyes were on them, till she noticed Marisol drop her raised hand.

"I was wondering why honour killings are described as a religious practice, and not as a cultural or social phenomena? And, besides, whose Islam are we talking about—I mean, does this family's background make a difference?"

Marisol had a clarity of mind and voice that never failed to impress Arubah. She felt the prof's gaze shift from Marisol to her, before answering: "Yes, well, those are important questions and best saved for next week's discussion."

Marisol persisted: "Yes, but if those practices are simply identified as Islamic, doesn't this put all Muslim Canadians under a microscope?"

Professor March reinstalled herself behind the podium, and started to gather her notes. "OK, class," she announced, "we can take up this and other questions after the midterm exam. Make sure you arrive at least five minutes early next week . . . And Happy Thanksgiving!"

Several students had already mobbed Professor March, who made a point of looking up at Arubah and Marisol on their way out.

"Tabarnak!" Marisol cursed, launching into a tirade against their prof's *evasive manoeuvres*.

Arubah decided it best to let Marisol vent. The grisly case of two teenage girls drowned in their car at the bottom of a river was hard enough to digest. And yet Professor March's reference to it was bothersome. She had even used the term "barbaric cultural practice" at one point in the lecture. This was the kind of language she expected from right-wing political camps, but not at university. Not from a professor she had come to admire.

They pushed open a massive door buttressed against a wind tunnel. As they acclimatized themselves to the world outside the lecture hall, Arubah noticed a guy standing against an old maple tree giving them a friendly wave.

"Someone you know?" she asked, hooking her arms through her backpack.

"Who?" Marisol looked up. "Oh yeah, he's just a guy in my Indigenous Theory course."

"He looks like he wants to say hi."

"Just keep walking." Marisol said and picked up the pace.

Arubah took bigger steps, and couldn't resist kicking up her foot, releasing a whorl of fallen leaves into the air. "I love this time of year!"

"Me too," Marisol contributed half-heartedly.

"Those were great questions, by the way. Just what I had in mind."

"Obviously not good enough! . . . *Take it up at after the midterm*, my ass! Next week is Thanksgiving, then midterms, and then we'll be onto a completely different subject!"

They walked along George Street towards Queen, each lost in the synaptic charge of their reflections. Arubah was beginning to see the seeds of a term paper emerge, and was about to tell Marisol as much when a girl with indigo streaks in her hair shouted out in passing: "Hey Marisol! Are you coming to the taskforce meeting tonight?"

"Yeah! Thanks for reminding me. What time is it again?" Marisol hollered, walking backwards a few paces.

"Eight! And we're going out for drinks after, so bring your game on!"

Arubah spent more time than needed zipping up her coat and retrieving her bus pass. It wasn't just that Marisol lived on campus and had a set of activities and friends that came with dormlife—she also belonged to that *other side*, which both she and Marisol seemed to keep at a safe distance from their friendship.

"Taskforce?" she felt compelled to inquire when the girl was out of earshot.

"Yeah, the LGBTQ+ reps are part of a campus-wide initiative on gender violence."

"Oh," Arubah lowered her head and noticed she'd walked right into a puddle.

"Still loving this time of year!" Marisol laughed.

Arubah shook some of the muddy water off her jeans. "You bet!"

They reached the point, not far from Marisol's dorm, where Arubah had to turn into the street to catch her bus. "Are we still on for Thanksgiving weekend?"

"Of course!" Marisol stopped and gave Arubah two light kisses, one on each cheek.

Arubah brightened. She was looking forward to Montreal, and she was curious to meet Marisol's parents, even though they seemed a bit intimidating. With a college prof and a legal advocate as parents, it was no wonder Marisol had a leg up over most of her student peers. It was no wonder she could go head-to-head with their profs! But the idea of spending Thanksgiving alone at home, with her mom still away in Pakistan, held far less appeal than a weekend with the Martinez-Hamids.

"I can't wait to show you around!" Marisol said. "Toronto's awesome but it's not Montreal!"

"So you keep saying!"

"And Elise is coming for dinner. I haven't seen her in . . . well, since forever."

Arubah's mood dampened. She knew Elise wasn't some random guest. She was Marisol's ex-girlfriend—a part of that *other side*.

"I think you'll like—" Marisol started.

"There's my bus!" Arubah looked up the street. "I'd better go!"

"We'll meet up at Union Station for Thanksgiving, then?" Marisol called after her.

"Yes—Union. See you then!"

3

Kashif watched his mother shuffling after the nurse. She really wasn't herself these days, hardly speaking to him at all or snapping at him for no good reason, as she'd done all the way to the hospital. It wasn't as if they were late—he had even left the mosque early, long before the cops came back on the wrecked scene. He had wanted to be there to hear if they had any leads. Instead, he had rushed home. He didn't even have time to change out of his sweats, though he was quite certain they had bits of glass stuck to them, but his mom didn't seem to notice any of that. She only managed to make some weird insinuations about his comings and goings—suspecting, he thought, that he was spending time with his dad behind her back. True, he didn't tell her much about his life these days, but there wasn't much to tell; and so what if he were meeting up with his dad?

One of the patients got up and fiddled with the television mounted on the wall. She wore a headscarf designed for chemo patients; he'd expected his mom to wear something similar, but she preferred a woolly toque, as if every season was winter.

"Would you like some help?" Kashif asked the woman by the TV.

"I'm looking for the volume control!" she said, looking up with relief.

"It's a touch-screen. Do you want to turn it up?"

"Yes, that would be nice!" she smiled appreciatively.

"No problem." Kashif adjusted the controls, and walked back to his seat, eager to start the latest version of *Grand Theft Auto*, downloaded on his phone for the long haul of his mom's appointments. He was a few minutes into the game when he caught an image on the TV. An attractive reporter with black-rimmed glasses and glossy hair was speaking into a large fuzzy microphone.

"Many volunteers, young and old, have worked tirelessly this morning, erasing the words 'No more refugees!' and 'Islam Must Die!' spray-painted in red on the mosque's exterior walls. The shards of glass from the broken windows have been cleared away, but it may be harder to calm the shattered nerves of a community still reeling from the effects of what appears to be just the latest in a string of attacks."

The camera panned across the scene, zooming into the broken windows that were now boarded up. The camera zoomed out, and Kashif sprang to his feet.

An older man, who was peering at the TV over his book, removed his reading glasses.

"You?" he asked, pointing to the guy dawdling behind the reporter and the distinguished, goateed man being interviewed.

Kashif nodded, a little embarrassed.

"We are standing here with Mr Ishaq Khan, the Director and Imam of the Islamic Cultural Centre, who has been speaking with the police since the last such incident. Mr Khan, the message here seems even more extreme than the first time this mosque was attacked. How do you think the Muslim community might respond to being targeted again?"

"Understandably, not just the Muslim community but also our friends and neighbours from the wider community are quite shaken by this attack and these messages. To see our holy book desecrated in this manner is particularly upsetting. But as Muslims, we are taught to love our neighbours and to work alongside them. In that spirit I would like to say we forgive whoever did this."

"Does that mean you don't wish to pursue an investigation or press charges in the event of an arrest?"

"We wish for dialogue. We invite whoever did this to let us answer some of the questions and concerns that led them to write such things

and burn the Quran."

"Mr Khan, is there any message that you would like to send the public today?"

"Only that we extend our deepest gratitude to the Rexdale community for their solidarity and support, as well as our young volunteers from the Islamic Cultural Centre who have come out to help us . . . "

The ads came on and Kashif sat down, embarrassed by his overexcitement.

"Those are some nasty messages," the older man commented.

"Yeah," Kashif said, noticing that the woman with the headscarf had dozed off.

"It's a good thing no one was hurt."

"But someone *could* have got hurt. Badly hurt!" Kashif mumbled. "It's just lucky no one was there at the time."

"Can't argue with you there."

Kashif fished out his phone, eager to resume the game.

"I'm Frank, by the way," he heard the man say.

"Kashif," he said, selecting a new avatar.

"It's a shame they aren't going to investigate."

Kashif hit "quicksave," and popped out his earbuds. "How do you know that?"

"Twenty-five years of service, young man! Ontario Provincial Police!" Frank winked. "Well, I'm out of commission for now, of course, on account of the Big-C. The reason we're all here, right?"

"That's cool. Not about the cancer! That's not cool. I meant the cop thing," Kashif sputtered. He'd been toying with the idea of applying to the police academy for the last few months.

"You disagree with him, don't you," Frank said.

"Sorry?"

"Just your expression when the Director was being interviewed."

"But I was only on TV for a few seconds—"

"I didn't mean on camera. I meant here, in the flesh!"

"Oh," Kashif said, shrinking into himself.

"Sorry—old habits." Frank returned to his book.

Kashif felt like he'd dishonoured Ishaq-bhai in some small but not insignificant way. Frustrated, he walked to the reception booth to see if his mother's appointment was over, but there was no sign of her or the receptionist.

The cop was thumbing through his book, so Kashif found a new seat perched right next to the floor-to-ceiling window that made the Princess Margaret so grand, with its polished floors and shiny gold plaques naming its wealthy donors and award-winning doctors. And that downtown view! Nothing could beat it, he always thought. He watched the bicycle couriers whizzing through the streets, the orderly traffic, how everything moved about with such purpose—so different from the suburbs, where highways, postage-stamp lawns, and strip-malls were all you could see. Nothing ever changed out there. Even his job at the gas station seemed to go nowhere. He'd been working there since high school. It put money in his pocket but it was never supposed to be a full-time job. It was on one of his night shifts that he'd been bored enough to start surfing the police academy website. He'd even downloaded a bunch of applications.

Kashif wondered if his dad could be somewhere in that moving traffic, on one of his taxi routes. Then he thought of the woman his dad was supposedly shacking up with. A part of him wished he didn't know any better, wished his dad would stop hounding him and just let him get on with his own life. Though he wasn't impressed with his mom either. How long would she have pretended everything was OK—that his dad had just "gone away for a while."

How had he not seen this coming? Was he more like his mom than he cared to admit, all shut off and closed down like a firewall against a virus? Volunteering at the Islamic Cultural Centre, which served Muslim Canadians of all backgrounds, was the first sociable thing he had done in ages. And he had only gone there at their neighbour Tasneem Aunty's prodding, to stay out of the house and let his mom rest. He didn't have any expectations of the Centre one way or another, but it was an impressive place with a new athletic wing. Tasneem Aunty had introduced him to Ishaq Khan or, as he was known at the Centre, Ishaq-bhai, a figure of considerable standing. It was Ishaq-bhai who encouraged him to volunteer, and before he knew it, the athletic facilities were less of an attraction than the chance to keep busy and hang out with some of the other volunteers—"boys your age," as Tasneem Aunty put it in her infinitely annoying way of speaking to him like a child. By the time he'd get home he was too tired to be depressed about his mom's illness, much less his dad's offenses.

Kashif caught Frank's imposing reflection in the glass as he came over. He may have been an older man, definitely older than his dad, but he didn't look like someone battling cancer. He looked like he could head up a Special Ops Unit or train a SWAT team. If this guy was anything to go by, Kashif doubted he'd ever make the cut.

"Just needed to stretch my legs a little," Frank said, looking out at the CN Tower rising above the Toronto skyline.

"Right," Kashif muttered.

"That man on TV—he's the Director of what, exactly?" Frank ventured.

"Sorry?"

"The gentleman being interviewed?"

"Oh, Ishaq-bhai? He's the Director of the Centre—the Islamic Cultural Centre. We call him an imam."

"Like a priest?"

"He does deliver sermons and all, but he's also seen as a community leader. Like today. He's the one who organized the cleanup, and he'll probably help the mosque find a way to pay for the damages. Anyway, I know him from the Centre."

"The Centre?"

"Like I said, the Islamic Cultural Centre in North York, not too far from where we—my mom and I—live. Most of us just call it the Centre. It's not a mosque, though it does hold some of the bigger religious prayer services. It's more like a community centre. A place to

18

hang out, volunteer, take classes—."

"Ah!" Frank stroked his chin. "So, do you think it's worth investigating—this latest attack?"

"Of course! Don't you?"

"Well, one never knows with these things. Most of the time it's just an attention-grabbing stunt. On the other hand, it could have the potential to escalate. Today, it was a rock through a window. Tomorrow, it could be . . . who knows."

"That's what I was thinking!" Kashif got up and stood next to Frank, confirming he was about a head shorter than the guy. "I mean, it's hardly an isolated incident—there've been quite a few attacks like this around the city. Not just buildings and vandalism but people have been attacked, too!"

"Sounds like you've been giving this a lot of thought."

"How can I *not* think about it! What if my mom was there! I mean, she doesn't really get out much these days, but you know what I mean—you think about this stuff when it hits home. When you're the target. Then, you have no choice but to think about it, I guess."

"Fair enough," Frank replied.

Kashif checked his watch. Sitting around in a place that reeked of bleach and disinfectant wipes had made him nauseous. He should have been used to it by now, but today it just got to him. It was all too perfect, too sterile, too clean. Today it just made him think of the little mosque where no amount of ammonia could wipe away the foulness of those words.

"That was your mom you're waiting on?" Frank said, taking a seat again.

"Yeah."

"How's she doing?"

"Not great . . . mouth cancer."

"That's a tough one, but Dr Eleniak's one of the best."

"He's your doctor, too?"

"Mm hmm."

"And you said you were a cop?" Kashif asked, emboldened by this unexpected connection.

Frank raised his eyebrows in the affirmative.

"Could I ask you something?" Kashif hedged. "About the police?"

"Try me." Frank tucked his book under his thigh.

"Would they take someone like me?"

"Depends on what you mean by 'someone like you'?" Frank replied. "Do you want to be a cop?"

"I don't know. I mean, yes. Maybe!"

A woman in a white lab coat entered the waiting room.

"Frank? Franklin Snyder?" she barked with a bit of an accent, making Kashif think of the number of times his mother had complained about the "Chinese" nurses because she had trouble understanding them. She much preferred the "other kind," which he took to mean Filipina, and at which point he would tune out, embarrassed by how racist she sounded.

"Yes, ma'am!" Frank looped his thumb in his belt.

"Follow me!" the woman commanded.

Kashif slumped back into his chair.

"Tell you what." Frank scratched his phone number onto one of the medical pamphlets fanned out on the table. "Call me if you decide how to answer that question!"

Kashif held up the pamphlet like a winning Lotto ticket. "Really?"

"Sure, why not!" Frank winked. "I've got a nose for these things."

"Thanks!" Kashif grinned.

"You're welcome . . . Kay-shift?"

"Close. Ka-shif."

"Sir!" the woman beckoned.

"Kar-chef. Got it!"

4

F rank Snyder pulled out of the hospital parking lot, giddy with the news he'd been waiting almost two years to hear. *Stopping at the log where catfish bite, walking along the river road at night,* he sang along with the radio as he came to a red light.

"Hey, if *you* just heard the words *complete remission,* you'd be singing at the top of your lungs too, lady!" he had the urge to roll down his window and shout at the woman in the car beside him.

The light turned green and Frank accelerated in step with the song.

Love to kick my feet way down the shallow water! he belted, transported to his own favourite spot at the Grand River—or the GR, as he liked to say, with his penchant for abbreviations.

He hadn't been fishing or canoeing in years, at least not since the Big-C, and certainly not along the GR, the slow-winding river that lay a hundred kilometres west of Toronto, cutting an impressive path from Lake Huron to Lake Erie. He'd walked along the ravines in the Don Valley, and had even caught a bit of the conservationist bug, going so far as taking one of those tours tracing "the lost rivers" of Toronto, which the guide had memorably described as "liquid phantoms" buried under cemeteries of concrete and steel. When it came down to it, though, nothing compared to the GR. It was the GR where his memories ran deepest.

Honking horns jolted Frank back to the river of bumper-to-bumper traffic on the Gardiner Expressway. Another siren, this time a police car, made him think of Wade, his old partner, and the rest of his buddies down at the OPP Sixth Division, his home away from home in the BTC, or Before-the-Cancer, years. They were a second family—though Cheryl had always bitched they were more like his first family, the one he'd grow old with. But, after an extended medical leave and the increasing likelihood that he might have to consider early retirement, he couldn't be sure who among the old gang was still there. By the time he'd left, it was already overrun by a new wave of recruits, including that girl, Nikita or Kiniesha—he couldn't keep track of these newfangled names. Still, he thought, it sure would be nice to tell Wade he'd licked the Big-C.

"Who'd have thunk it!" Frank had said to Dr Eleniak on hearing the news that morning.

"You're a champ, Frank! Complete remission is rare with a late diagnosis." Dr Eleniak gave his patient a friendly pat on the shoulder.

"So, it's done? I'm good to go?" Frank said disbelievingly.

"Onto big and bold adventures!" the doctor said like a teacher at a graduation ceremony. "But first, please take time to celebrate!"

"Celebrate," Frank echoed. He would have liked nothing more than to celebrate with Cheryl and Chris. He'd take everyone out for a big fat juicy steak. But that was in the BTD, or Before-the-Divorce, years. Cheryl had moved on with some corporate-type she had met online.

As for his son Chris, all he could do was leave messages and hope he'd take time out of his precious day to get back to the MWGHL, or the Man-Who'd-Given-Him-Life, as Frank referred to himself whenever his son got under his skin, which was proving to be a chronic condition of late. Chris showed no interest in anything—anything except those *dang* video games he played 24-7, the kind that came with trigger warnings. And those gigantic headphones were melded onto his head, turning him into a creature from an old Star Trek episode. If he didn't know any better, Frank would say his kid had an addiction. He could barely come up for air, even on Frank's infrequent visits. And he wasn't even sure if Chris was holding down a job. For a while he thought he could groom him for the trades but that had proved to be an exercise in futility. The last time he had managed to get two words out of him, Chris said he had quit a part-time job at Taco Bell. He vividly recalled the deadpan stare he got in return for having dared ask what he planned to do next.

Why hadn't Cheryl seen fit to boot their son out of the house by now, Frank burned. She had seen fit to kick *him* out two years ago, right in the midst of his treatments! She'd been heartless enough to leave a drowning man to die when it suited her, hadn't she? But she continued to coddle that golden boy of hers, using *his* house to keep his son from growing the hell up!

Someone speeding in a white Audi flashed by Frank's blind spot.

"Goddamn FOBs!" Frank hurled, convinced that a new wave of immigrants were the worst traffic offenders because, as he'd tell the guys at the Division, they'd only recently traded in their bicycles for sports cars, which always got a good rise out of them—everyone but Nashika, or whatever her name was.

Maybe it was just as well he'd taken a break from it all, Frank sighed in retrospect. What was it that Wade said the last time they'd hung out for a beer? "Times have changed like you wouldn't believe, Frank. You can't so much as breathe without some chick accusing you of sexual harassment, much less make a joke without it being turned into a federal offense! I'd be celebrating if I had the chance to get out early—not to say you haven't been through the ringer, pal, but you know what I mean . . ."

Sadly, Frank did know what Wade meant. He knew *exactly* what Wade meant. That he was yesterday's news, with or without the Big-C. That his authority counted for shit. His son was living proof of that. Still, another part of him liked to think he was man enough to face whatever these changing times had to throw at him. Sure, he still carried around some of his own baggage, but he wasn't so out of step with things. If anything, he considered himself a far sight more enlightened than most other guys at the Division, even the newbies, always bracing himself for the day a domestic disturbance call would end up at one of *their* doorsteps.

Wade was wrong about one thing though—there was nothing to celebrate about being away from the thing he loved most in this world: policing.

Frank exited the 427 with no more CCR to buoy his spirits, and pulled up to a putty-beige twenty-storey that had come to have the sorry title of *home* in the ATD, or After-the-Divorce years. Its tired eighties construction stood out like a bad weed among the show-pieces sprouting up around Etobicoke. An elderly driver was making a turtle-like exit out of the underground parking lot, so Frank idled at the top of the driveway, focused on the black void beyond the narrow entrance as she passed. When the garage door started to close behind her, Frank couldn't get himself to reactivate it. Wrapping a clammy hand around the gearshift, he put the car in reverse with an unexpected surge of adrenaline.

A few minutes later he was back on the 427, rubbing a bead of sweat off his brow. An attractive woman in a Lexus SUV shot him a sideways glance when he found himself cruising beside her, her brown face and jet-black hair reminding him of that boy in the hospital, Kar-shift or Kay-chef, whose interest in the police had really cheered him up.

He kept pace with the Lexus as they came within sight of the highway's notorious split, forcing drivers to make last-minute lane changes at their own peril. Frank figured the woman would speed past him to head west to Mississauga or Milton—the new Little Indias, as they liked to call them, only these boroughs were the size of some of Canada's major cities now. The woman stayed in her lane, which meant she was probably heading north or maybe even east, which was also populated by all kinds of minorities—Indian, Chinese, Caribbean, Iranian. Though, truth be told, he was the one who felt like a minority the last time he was out there.

He and the Lexus driver decelerated at the same rate. Frank wanted to buy himself some time, unsure where he was heading. West could take him back to Kitchener. How long had it been since he'd tried to get back out there? They used to drive up a few times a year for the annual Oktoberfest and the odd family gathering, but now he rarely found a reason to make the trip.

When Cheryl got the opportunity to transfer to a bigger hospital as a triage nurse and Chris had just completed his last year before Junior High, it had seemed like the perfect time to make the BM, the Big Move, to Toronto. Besides, Cheryl hadn't needed any convincing: she was born in Toronto and hated Kitchener which, as she never ceased to remind him, smelled of pig farms and industrial waste. He had no idea what she was on about, considering most of the farms were lost to housing developments and the old industries had become hip IT companies, but the imagery had its desired effect. Frank could see it was time to move, if only because of the old adage, Happy Wife, Happy Life.

Frank reckoned he hadn't returned to Kitchener since the last Thanksgiving family dinner. He would have made an effort, if only for his sister Emmy's sake, but she had moved on too, heading out West with a mechanical engineer at one of those big oil companies in Alberta. Frank was really happy for her, considering how hard she'd worked all those years, putting Brittany through school as a single mom. He wondered what his niece was up to now. The last time they'd spoken, Brittany was still living in Kitchener, but Emmy didn't elaborate. Maybe Brittany had got back together with that guy Joey from the Six Nations. His name had kept coming up at dinner, much to his sister's irritation. Though he had been glad of it, since it gave the "Great Flood-talk," a staple at family dinners, a much-needed rest.

A siren alerted the cars to move to the shoulder as an ambulance forged its way to the Islington North exit. Frank tailed the ambulance, figuring time would be far better spent at a coffee shop over sitting in traffic for no good reason, especially since his walk down memory lane had made him realize he hadn't eaten a thing since breakfast.

Rollin', rollin' . . . Frank sang, feeling cheered again, cheered enough to think that maybe Wade could be persuaded to join him for a bite. It had been too long. Far too long.

When a parking lot presented itself, he pulled over to make the call, relieved to get off the road for a few minutes. He looked idly about as Wade's phone rang, his gaze landing on a small group of men amassed outside a building on the other side of the street. They were wearing traditional clothes. The building looked familiar, too. It looked like the scene of "the attack"—the one on the morning news.

Frank pushed the thought aside as Wade's phone went to voicemail. He hung up and tried again, though the people across the street still held his attention. A handful of men were milling about, as others hauled buckets and other hardware away. The damage appeared far greater than the cursory shots of a broken window he had caught on the local news. The whole exterior had taken a beating, starting with a door dangling off its hinges. And the place would need a pretty major facelift, almost every inch of it covered in blood-red spray paint.

"Screw this!" Frank dropped the line before he had to hear Wade's wife's nasally voice again.

He made a U-turn to get back home, but found himself pulling into the parking lot at the side of the vandalized building. It was hardly as if he had anything better to do.

5

Kauthar Siddiqui was bulldozed by her appointment with Dr Eleniak. She hadn't budged from the living room sofa since getting back home from the hospital with Kashif, who was now sitting opposite her, immersed in a phone conversation. A film was playing on one of the satellite TV channels but all she could focus on was the doctor's dim prognosis. She had learned that she was not yet ready to be relieved of the feeding tube inserted in her stomach, which meant she had to put up with more pain and embarrassment. For how long? The torment was enough to make her want to cry.

"The news? . . . Yeah, I watched it at the hospital," Kashif was saying.

Kauthar turned to the film, hoping it might lift her spirits. The romantic winter scene took her back to a childhood trip to Murree, the mountain resort town in northern Pakistan. She would never have imagined that one day she would be living in one of the snowiest places on earth. Though, in this city, snow solidified into blackened mounds at the edge of multilane highways—hardly anything like the serene place she remembered from her childhood.

"Yeah, it was cool being on TV, I guess. But it's too bad they didn't interview the maulana. He may not have been as diplomatic as Ishaqbhai . . . Yeah, at least no one got hurt, Allah ke fazal . . . "

Kauthar stirred on hearing her son use the phrase "Allah ke fazal." Saying "Thank God," was one thing. But Allah ke fazal? He had never spoken that way before. All pious and proper. And why was he inquiring after a maulana? They hadn't been to a mosque in years. For that matter, who was this Ishaq-bhai? The name was vaguely familiar. Had Kashif mentioned it before or did she know it from somewhere else? She was increasingly bothered by the fact that her son was spending less and less time at home, and more and more time away. It was too much like the months before . . . She felt the heat rise to her face and, with it, the pain.

"*Nasser* wants us to meet him? . . . Why?" Kashif continued. "Are you going?"

The boy showed no signs of getting off the phone, and Kauthar settled on watching the film. It was called *Ram Teri Ganga Maili*, followed by the English translation, *Ram, Your Ganges is Dirty*, cast in red letters across the screen. The South Asian channels helped her get through days that unfolded with the certainty of sickness and inertia. But she missed going to work at the Ginetti Family Food Corporation. She even felt a brief twinge of nostalgia for Indira, her disagreeable supervisor. She had worked there a long time now. How long was it?

"Too-too many years!" her Bangladeshi neighbour Tasneem Baksh always preached. "Kauthar, why don't you get a job closer to home!" Easy for Tasneem to say! She hadn't worked a day in her life.

The doctor had said it would be a while before she was "out of the woods"—another one of those Canadian expressions she had relied on Kashif to explain. Only this one had stuck because she had come to think of her face as a mountain beaten down by a landslide after monsoon season. At least that's what she saw now that a section of her oral cavity, as they called it, was cut out to prevent the cancer from spreading.

"The letter? . . . Yeah, Nasser mentioned it but, come to think of it, no one else said much about it. Not even Ishaq-bhai." Kashif's voice weaved in and out of the film's dramatic musical score. "OK, sure. I have to run a quick errand at the Centre tomorrow, but I can bus it out from there."

A weight pressed down on the sofa cushion, igniting little stabbing sensations on the right side of Kauthar's face. It was Kashif looking for the remote.

He fished it out and resumed his position on the armchair. "I have to change the channel, Ammi."

"... *This was the second act of vandalism against the Masjid Omar Bin Al-Hamad ... The police have only confirmed that the incident will be given their full attention ... In other news, grocery stores are running out of frozen turkeys for Thanksgiving faster than they can restock them ...*"

Kashif was addicted to the news, just like his father was. Kauthar didn't mind watching news now that so many anchors looked "hum log ki jaisey." More like us. More like her. If she plugged her ears and only watched, she was instantly transported back to Pakistan. If she closed her eyes and only listened, there was no difference between them and the goras, the white news anchors.

The light from the television illuminated Kashif's jawline as he switched channels, stopping at whichever news station he could find. If it weren't for the stubble on his unshaven face, he was a spitting image of his father. Hassan Siddiqui was a good-looking man. Everyone had said so at their wedding, the cutting insinuation about the obvious mismatch between the newly-weds still as hurtful as the first time it was delivered by relatives, near and distant. And now even more so, with cancer and surgery, while he was gallivanting around with another woman—a white woman. A gori!

The medical team at the Princess Margaret were always so concerned about physical changes, constantly reminding her of the counseling and rehabilitation available for patients undergoing invasive surgeries. But she wouldn't know what to do or say at these sessions. All that talk about body image seemed a waste of time. She'd spent her best years wearing factory coats and hair netting, while also caring for husband and child; there was hardly any time to worry about how she looked. When Kashif was younger, they had attended a few functions, which were always fun to dress up for, but that was in their early years as new arrivals. Their *honeymoon* years, when she was foolish enough to think that being separated from everything familiar—her sisters, her family, her air, her sky—would be worth it. For this marriage. For Hassan.

Kauthar saw that Kashif had switched the TV back to the movie channel before disappearing into his room. She wondered what plans he had just made for tomorrow. She considered asking Tasneem to help keep an eye on him. But Kashif was a young man, not a child. Besides, any contact with Tasneem came at a steep price. First, it meant having to hear her neighbour's ministrations about this-that-or-the other. And second, it meant overlooking the fact that Tasneem had been avoiding her. Even though no one spoke about it openly, she was certain that word had got out about Hassan's shameful behaviour.

In her more forgiving moments, Kauthar tried not to hold this obvious snub against her neighbour. She understood that Tasneem didn't wish to be tarnished by scandal, even if only by association. She had her standing in the community to uphold, always flaunting the fact that they were hajis, having made the pilgrimage to Mecca, and that they had lived in Saudi Arabia for several years before coming to Canada. If anything, Kauthar envied Tasneem's piety, attributing to it her many blessings, including her beautiful twin daughters, Bina and Banu.

Kauthar had always longed for a second child, a little sister for Kashif. She wondered what it would be like to raise a girl here. Would she turn out like Bina and Banu in their long black robes? Would she turn out like Abena, the daughter of her Sudanese neighbour, Mrs Osman, who had dyed her hair blonde and wore clothes so tight it was a wonder she could breathe? Or would she turn out like her younger co-worker Arubah, in jeans and hijab, whom Kauthar likened to apple chutney, a Canadian adaptation of a familiar staple.

Arubah was one of the youngest workers at Ginetti's, and yet *she* had stood up to Indira, their supervisor, with nerves as sharp as those industrial machines. Kauthar assumed that Arubah's confidence came from all the choices and opportunities this younger generation—the children of immigrants—seemed to have. At least Arubah wasn't wasting those opportunities! She was going to the top university, which Hassan had always hoped Kashif would attend—on this point, at least, she and her husband were united. It was Kashif who was the odd one out, complaining he didn't want to become some suited-booted banker-type, as if that was the only thing people went to university for! What about Arubah? Kauthar didn't quite recall what her co-worker was studying but it was clear how hard she worked to put herself through university. If she could do it, then why couldn't their son!

Kauthar sighed, impressed but also a little envious of young women like Arubah. It was Arubah who had the courage, without a trace of ridicule or judgment, to confirm Kauthar's worst suspicions about Hassan and *that woman*. Kauthar couldn't believe that was a year ago now—the same day Arubah had it out with Indira.

Arubah had been running a little late that day. Kauthar didn't think much of this until she heard her younger co-worker's voice soaring above the clank and drone of the machinery. But it was the content and not the pitch of Arubah's outpouring that seemed all the more remarkable: "You're OK with robbing us of a few minutes pay! But overtime for extra long shifts—*that's* too much to ask for! And we all know there are at least a dozen health violations in this place that you don't report, Indira! So, suspend me, fire me—do whatever you want—because it will give me time to let the Ministry of Labour hear all about our working conditions!"

The workers stopped what they were doing and looked on, open-mouthed and stunned, as their supervisor fixed a hawkish eye on Arubah.

"Arré! Who gave you all permission to stop working!" Indira eventually barked before skulking away into her makeshift office.

Everyone turned back to their stations, pretending to be engrossed in their mundane tasks. Kauthar was no exception, her hands at the ready to pick up anything that looked burned or misshapen and throw it into the "reject" bin. If the biscuit didn't have a perfect "S" shape or looked more brown than golden, it had to be discarded. She was horrified by such wastefulness, and even tried to salvage the discards—at least the birds could enjoy them—but Indira said anything taken out of the factory was tantamount to corporate theft!

Arubah had taken her place on the assembly line beside Kauthar, but she didn't say anything until after the lunch break, after her usual prattle about her studies at the university.

"To tell you the truth, Aunty-ji, I don't feel safe waiting for the bus after my evening classes anymore," Arubah said, referring to the escalation of sexual assaults on campus. "Just the other day a student was attacked, steps from my department!" Then she tapped Kauthar's shoulder and with lowered voice said: "Kauthar Aunty, there's something I have to tell you."

Kauthar assumed this had to do with Arubah's altercation with their supervisor and didn't want to get involved. But Arubah prodded, "Aunty-ji."

"Achha—jaldi batao," Kauthar prompted her to be quick about it, looking around to ensure Indira or her lackeys were not within earshot.

"Aunty-ji, you know how Indira was mad at me because I was late this morning?"

"Yes?"

"Well, I lost it earlier because I had tried to explain why I was late—that I had to drop off a paper at the university, all the way downtown, before coming to work."

"It's too much for you, all this back and forth between work and the university."

"That's true, Aunty-ji. I'm not sure how much longer I can keep it up. But, anyway, that wasn't my point. I just wanted to tell you that while I was downtown, I saw something—I mean, *someone*."

Kauthar stepped back from the assembly line, grasping a handful of broken biscuits.

"Aunty-ji," Arubah gently squeezed Kauthar's arm to hold her attention. "I think—I'm pretty sure—it was Hassan. I mean, it was your husband, Hassan, walking by the campus. I just thought I'd mention it because he wasn't alone. He was *with* someone . . . "

Kauthar tossed the broken biscuits into the reject bin, a sign for Arubah to stop before she got herself into her second altercation of the day.

On her bus ride home, Kauthar tried to visualize Hassan *with someone*. She knew all too well what Arubah had been getting at. She had known it but she just couldn't get herself to say it. But now, with Arubah's information, things looked far more serious than she had imagined, the opprobrious glares at her wedding coming back to haunt her like an eerie prophecy. There was so much temptation for men here. All these girls wearing so little—in sun or snow. Girls like Abena, Mrs Osman's daughter. She imagined him talking to them on his taxi routes, especially late at night when they were drunk and felt less threatened by a brown man holding their life in his hands.

Kauthar didn't know what else to do but go on with her life as normal. How else could she save face? She made a vow never to speak a word about her illness, or anything else that mattered, to her husband, that good-for-nothing, ever again.

"Ammi! . . . Ammi, wake up!"

Kauthar looked up with a start, wondering why Hassan was wearing that forest-green sweater, the one she had bought for Kashif last Christmas.

"Ammi!" Kashif repeated, turning off the television.

The room fell silent save for a bird's twittering on the balcony ledge. Kauthar couldn't ignore the bird's call, and reached for Kashif's uneaten crust, dislodging a loose stack of colourful pamphlets in the process. A few were from the Cancer Society, which the nurse had plied her with on their last visit. She had said something about newly implemented on-line chat groups, but Kauthar didn't know the first thing about computers, much less how to talk to complete strangers about such private things. She was about to throw them away when another pamphlet titled "Islamic Cultural Centre" above the image of a glass-encased building, with a large steel dome off to one side, grabbed her attention. She recalled Tasneem talking about this place incessantly, like it was the Taj Mahal or Mecca, itself. The Islamic Cultural Centre boasted the usual kinds of things, like wedding venues and schedules for Quranic classes, but also unexpected things like sports facilities and fitness studios for women, and even family counseling services.

She set down the pamphlets, unnerved by the striking contrast between this shiny new complex and that dingy room in a strip mall plaza, with its musty carpets and cramped quarters, which had served as a mosque in the early days when they still made an effort to attend religious service.

The twittering increased, the lone sparrow joined by her clan and a couple of mourning doves, all lined up on the balcony ledge in hungry anticipation.

"Mein arrahi hun, chhoti parinda!" Kauthar assured the birds she was on her way.

6

Arubah flashed her student bus pass and took the first available seat. She didn't have class today and had offered to help out with Tariq al-Nur, or Path-to-Light, a campaign addressing domestic violence in the Muslim community. The campaign was the initiative of Dr Mona Ali, the Director of Family Counseling at the Islamic Cultural Centre, where Arubah was headed for the day.

Arubah's mom, Raim Anwar, had pestered her to drop either the volunteer work at the Centre or her job at Ginetti's, concerned that both were a distraction from studies during her senior year. But her mom changed her tune about the Centre when it looked like she had to fly to Pakistan on account of Arubah's grandfather's ailing health. Apparently, more time spent at the Centre meant more opportunities for the *aunties* to look out for Arubah while she was away. Arubah joked that these so-called aunties had better things to do than check up on her, but she couldn't disagree that it was time to let go of her job at Ginetti's. She had already reduced her shifts to the bare minimum, and it hardly seemed worth the commute anymore.

Arubah wondered how her grandfather was doing. The last time they spoke her mom said it wasn't looking good, which was why she had dropped everything to be there for his "final days." The fact that her mom hadn't been able to say goodbye to Arubah's dad in *his* final days still cut her deeply. Javid Anwar had died on the operating table, the victim of a head-on collision on the 401—on what should have been another ordinary drive home from the office.

Arubah took a deep breath at the memory. After her dad's death, everything in their lives had moved at an accelerated rate. Her mom went back to work, getting a job in retail; she sold the bulk of their furniture and downsized to a cramped townhouse better suited to a "family of two," as she had come to refer to them. "I'm not a single mom!" she would rant at no one in particular. "I'm a widow. There's a difference!" Arubah would object that there was no shame in that, but her mom insisted she was not ashamed, saying, "When people call me a single mom it's as if your father never existed. And I can't accept that! I just can't!"

It was almost thirteen years since her father's death. It was hard not to feel like the kid of a single mom when memories of her dad were confined to digital photos, half-remembered phrases, and feelings trapped in the haze of childhood. The truth was that they had been a *family of two* since she was ten—longer than they had been anything else.

Arubah wished the bus would speed up, regretting she had never got round to getting a driver's license, probably because her mom had sworn off driving after the accident. Though, for Arubah, even driving was just one of many forfeited rites of passage. She even got through high school like it was a four-year detention period. Her mom had tried to make a fuss over graduation, urging her to accept a date for the prom because that was *how it was done around here*, but Arubah couldn't see herself all dolled up for a desi guy whose mom called her mom to set up the date! If anything, Arubah wasn't as eager to accept *how things were done around here*. Would her dad have been so eager? Would he have approved of her dating guys before puberty or parading around in spaghetti-strapped gowns that looked like lingerie? Would he have approved of pajama parties that were just a cover-up for make-out sessions with boyfriends? Every part of what was *done around here* screamed *betrayal* to the memory of her dad! Couldn't her mom see that? Why couldn't she consider what her dad would have wanted? Wasn't this overly liberal style of parenting another way of *erasing him*?

Arubah rubbed her temple, a headache coming on from the incessant tittering produced by a group of teenagers sitting somewhere behind her. She had already done a quick sweep of the bus, noticing the teenagers, a handful of seniors, a few loners, and a woman in burqa. She had noticed the woman because of the child, a boy of no more than four or five, pressed up against her. She used to be that child, all burrowed into her mom because she was perennially cold, even in the summer. But her dad's death had the strange effect of making her both more dependent on her mom and more self-reliant, and now part of her relished having the house all to herself while the other part couldn't bear the silence.

The bus crossed an overpass, and she could see they were already in North York. She closed her eyes for the last stretch of the trip, hoping it would help block out the teenagers, who were only getting louder at every turn.

"You hiding a bomb under there, or what?" Arubah thought she heard one of them say. Alarmed, she turned around and saw the teenagers heckling the woman in burqa.

"Yeah, like a missile or two!" one of the two girls joined in.

"More like a good hard missile right between the—"

"Ew! Should I be jealous, Cole!"

Arubah saw the child tremble and the woman pulled him even closer; she snuck a look at the back of the bus which had cleared out at the last few stops, save for a few of the seniors.

"Gross!" the guy called Cole snorted. "She looks like a walking coffin!"

"Like, why the fuck do they come here if they don't want to be free!"

"I don't even think that covering your face like that is legal here, is it?" the other girl across the aisle said, almost studiously, as if she'd been reading up on the proposed bans on Islamic head-coverings in public spaces.

"Yeah! Like the driver shouldn't have let Darth Vader on the bus!" Cole thrust himself over the chair the child was sitting on.

"It creeps me out!" the girlfriend said, rubbing her arms. "Someone should tell her to take it off!"

"Take it off! Take it off! Take it off!" Cole chanted, drumming the back of the child's chair.

When Arubah heard whimpering she could take it no more. "Can't you see you're upsetting this poor child?"

"Look, Ash! They're cloning themselves!" Cole slumped back and draped a lazy arm around his girlfriend.

Arubah made a point of walking up to them this time: "Apologize to this woman immediately or I'm calling the cops!"

"Oooh, I'm scared!" Cole pushed his leg out into the aisle, forcing Arubah to take a step back.

"Like Kay said, *you're* the illegals!" Ash looked over to the girl across the aisle, but she had shrunk into herself and turned away.

"FYI, racial harassment is a crime, so the only people breaking any laws are you three losers!"

Arubah clasped the overhead bar as the bus made a sharp turn, bringing the Centre, which was perched on a slight incline, into view. She could get off soon but what about the woman and child? She took a chance and spoke to her in Urdu, figuring she was from Bangladesh or Pakistan. The woman understood and moved to the front of the bus where the driver could keep an eye on things.

Arubah wanted to look back and give the teenagers the finger, but she resisted out of consideration for the woman and child. She breathed easy as the bus pulled away and she started walking uphill, but it wasn't long before laughter and catcalls trailed after her.

"Hey, wait up, bitch!" Cole's voice led the charge.

"How come you're walking all by your lonesome?" Arubah heard the girlfriend, Ash, call out. "Your man let you off his leash?"

"Who let the dogs out! Woof woof woof!" Cole started up, wildly off-tune.

Arubah looked down at the dandelions poking through the cracks in the pavement, willing herself to react, to yell, to scream. But that other Arubah—the one with a voice—had disappeared with the bus. She had been caterwauled before, she rationalized. A man had thrown an empty beer bottle at her from an apartment balcony once. This was more of the same. Just more of the same.

Arubah kept going but she could still hear them cussing. "Alhamdulillah," she prayed in quiet gratitude when a large dome came into view, its steel façade catching the glint of the sun.

"Just do it, Kay!" Arubah heard Ash shout.

"Shut up, Ash!" Cole shushed her. "Kay's got this!"

Arubah turned, ever so slightly, coming face to face with *her*, the girl she had foolishly misconstrued as the studious one, the one who'd averted her gaze from Arubah, as if to distance herself from the others.

"Kay! Kay! Kay!" Ash and Cole spurred her on, and she grabbed the back of Arubah's hijab. With a second vicious tug the fabric shifted and tightened against her ear. Arubah let out a cry and Kay retreated into congratulatory howls of "Fuckin' A!" and "You bad ass!"

Arubah was trembling by the time she caught a glimpse of her reflection in the Centre's revolving glass doors. One side of her hijab was perfectly intact, while the other had come undone, flapping around like a flag at half-mast. She would have laughed at the ridiculous image were it not for her pounding heart and burning ear. She touched it to make sure it wasn't bleeding and realized something was off. Her earring. One of the precious gold hoops—the last gift from her dad. Gone.

Arubah jumped at the sensation of a hand on her bent elbow.

"I'm so sorry! I didn't mean to scare you!"

Arubah removed the hand from her ear and saw a face emerge like developing film in a photographer's lab.

"Arubah, right? We know each other, don't we?" A guy about her age was staring at her under bushy brows and a mop of wavy hair, a clump sitting like paisley print on his forehead.

"Kashif?"

"You worked with my mom, right? I've seen you around here a lot, but—"

"I know! I mean, yes! I worked with Kauthar Aunty—I mean your mom!" Arubah said, still disoriented. "How is she?"

"She's doing OK, thanks. Anyway, I'm sorry, I just thought I'd say hi—"

"Oh God!" she scrambled to fix the unfastened hijab. "I must look crazy!"

"Of course not!" Kashif smiled with his eyes, she noticed.

"I think . . . I think I was just assaulted . . . " The words gushed out of her like water from the campus faucet while Kashif listened patiently, intently. She and Kashif had never talked, except for the briefest of introductions when he'd picked up his mom at the factory once, and yet here she was, baring her soul, as if they had known each other forever.

Arubah felt herself being guided to the bench in the main hall. Then Kashif stepped away and reappeared with a glass of water.

"My earring," she said, gulping down the water. "I think it fell when . . . God, I have to find it!"

"What does it look like?"

Arubah started to describe it but jumped to her feet when she realized what time it was. Her meeting would be well underway by now.

"I'm sorry, I have to go!" she called out to the bewildered face staring at her as the elevator doors closed.

7

Kashif scanned Al's Roti Hut menu board tacked behind the cash counter. Doubles, Pholourie, Jerk Chicken, he went down the list of Caribbean dishes. He wondered if he had made the right call, trusting that kid he had met at the Centre to give Arubah the earring. He had searched high and low for it, going all the way to the bus stop and back, and now he was late for Nasser's meeting. He had wanted to ask for her number, but didn't know if that would be improper or uncool. What if she thought he was taking advantage of the situation—*of her*! Besides, she wasn't just any girl. He couldn't just call her up out of the blue—suppose she was ultra-orthodox? But surely, they could meet up for a coffee without it having to be seen as a newsbreaking scandal! But then again, he'd barely navigated the regular dating scene much less one controlled by the Muslim auntie-surveillance network, as some of the guys at the Centre joked. To be fair, he wouldn't even be at the Centre if Tasneem Aunty hadn't poked her nose into his business and talked up the place. He didn't have much in common with the more conservative types, but the Centre had a way of making people feel connected. Even perfect strangers. Though he and Arubah weren't strangers. They knew each other, *kind of*—or at least he'd caught himself noticing her too many times to count, kicking himself for not approaching her when he had a perfectly good ice-breaker: her acquaintance with his mom. If their paths hadn't crossed today, he knew his track record well enough to figure he'd go on noticing her without doing anything about it.

For the first time in his life luck was on his side—like the universe was opening just a fraction of a crack. But he quickly reminded himself that his good day was Arubah's bad day. She was attacked, for God's sake, and here he was all caught up with his own crap. At least if he could have stayed behind and accompanied her home, he would have felt a lot better.

"Have a seat!" Kashif heard Nasser wave him over to a table at the back of the largely empty restaurant, the lunch crowd having already dispersed. It looked like he'd called a bunch of other guys to this meeting.

"You know everyone here, right?" Nasser asked, his suit still plastered to him like a billboard announcing his newly minted business degree.

"Uh, sure." He was vaguely acquainted with Ismail and Omar, but only Zafar was someone he considered a friend. It usually took him a long time to open up to people, but Zafar beat him to it, rambling off his life story during their first encounter. Unlike Kashif's parents, who had taken a one-way ticket from Karachi to Toronto, on account of it being the *Desi* mecca, the Salims had landed in Quebec and later settled in Ontario. As Zafar recounted it, one day his father told them to pack whatever they could stuff into a rented minivan and drove them to what he called the "big English city with the giant tower." Eventually, the harrowing drive across the TransCanada highway in a winter snow squall paid off: Zafar's father landed a job with a German pharmaceutical company that didn't have any hang-ups about hiring a Muslim man with expertise in biochemicals, or at least that's how Zafar joked about it. Zafar's family lived in a big house in Mississauga now, unlike Kashif and his mom, who had never made it out of their North York apartment. But Kashif appreciated the fact that Zafar wasn't a snob, like some of the other guys at the Centre—the kind his dad described as entitled offspring of the land-owning families of the East who still behaved like masters in the West, where there was no one to lord it over but each other.

"Achha!" Nasser acknowledged in Urdu, though not everyone could understand the mother tongue he and Kashif shared. Ismail's parents had immigrated to Canada from Somalia, and Omar's family had roots in India from way back, but he was born somewhere in East Africa. That's why he'd grown up speaking Swahili. He wasn't sure about a few of the other guys at the table.

"This is Jamshed," Nasser said, pointing to an unshaven guy wearing a Moto jacket, black jeans, and a vintage t-shirt.

"It's Jam," Jamshed mumbled without looking up from his phone.

"And this is my cousin Arif visiting from Dubai," Nasser gestured toward a kid wearing eye glasses and slurping a nonalcoholic ginger beer.

"And finally, this is Kamal," Nasser said of the guy who both did and didn't look like *one of them*—whatever that meant.

"Hi," Kamal said amiably.

"Kamal's dad owns this place! *Al* is code for *Ali*, right Kamal?"

Kamal explained, almost apologetically, that his father wanted to call the place Ali's Roti Hut but some guy from Trinidad had beaten him to it, so he settled for Al, even though he didn't like Anglicized names.

"Well, the food here is great, yaar! Hundred-percent halal!" Nasser commented like an ad-exec. "It's a little out of the way but that's probably a good thing today," he added cryptically.

"The menu looks great!" Kashif said, his stomach growling.

"Kamal's from Ghana," Arif sputtered through a mangled straw.

"Not Ghana, you goofball!" Nasser flicked a clump of Arif's hair. "*Guy*-ana!"

Kashif smiled, thinking it would have been nice to have a "goofball" younger brother like Arif.

"How did your family end up all the way there?" Ismail asked.

Kashif liked the way Ismail's narrow face expanded with curiosity. He seemed like a nice guy, but he had never hung out with him before.

"My dad's grandparents went there as indentured labourers—you know, like the guys who come here from Mexico to work on the farms," Kamal explained. "And my mom's family were Indonesians who ended up in Suriname, though her mother was half-Dutch. So, we're Caribbean, South American, Asian, *and* European!"

"Ah!" Ismail looked satisfied that the mystery surrounding Kamal's distinctive features had been solved.

"Is that them?" Arif pointed at some prints on the mango-coloured walls.

"Arré! Don't be an idiot!" Nasser scoffed but took a moment to appraise the wall art.

"Those are just pictures poached from the Tourism Board. But my dad was born not far from that place." Kamal gestured at a picture with blue boats in a muddy river. "That's the Demerera river, the biggest and longest in Guyana, I think."

"Are there anacondas there?" Arif smushed his glasses against his face.

"My dad never saw one but my grandparents caught one in the rice paddies on their farm. My family has a picture of it. It's massive! Almost fifteen feet."

"No shit?" Jamshed contributed, his curiosity finally piqued enough to look up.

"Yeah, but the anacondas aren't the biggest threat. It's the smaller, venomous snakes that you really have to watch out for. Like the bushmaster and the coral."

"What are you lads talking about?" A middle-aged man strode over to the table, his belly protruding through an apron bearing the phrase, 'Never trust a skinny chef!'

"Hi, Dad. I was telling them about the snakes in Guyana!"

"Oh boy! We've got all kinds of strange creatures back home!" Ali said with an accent that was almost identical to one of Kashif's old high school teachers, Ms Coopsammy.

Everyone turned their attention from the wall art to the apron-sporting man.

"Must have been strange enough to bring all those famous explorers like Sir Walter Raleigh there, right? Only those guys, with their funny hats and tights, used to make up all kinds of rubbish about the place for the benefit of their *royal* patrons!" Ali took a mock bow with his kitchen rag. "Making all those far-flung places look so dark and mysterious was just good business back then, I suppose."

"Why?" Arif said, enthralled.

"Because, young man, you can't *pretend* to save a people from a place that looks quiet and peaceful! Saving a place from demons and demagogues sounds so much the nobler enterprise!" Ali draped the rag across his right shoulder, resting a liberated hand against the back of his son's chair. "Truth be told there was no need for exaggeration. Guyana's got its own special qualities—a kind of deep magical power that's never needed," he stopped for effect, "no *fake news!*"

Ismail and Omar snickered, and Kamal explained, "Dad was a journalist before he came to Canada."

"No, son! I was not a journalist *before* I came to Canada. It's not something you become and then *un-become*! Once you're a doctor, aren't you always a doctor? You'd still be called on to save lives if you had to, right?"

Everyone nodded in polite agreement. It was an unspoken rule of deference to an elder they all shared, which was one reason Kashif felt so at home in the company of guys from the Centre—guys he hadn't even grown up with.

"Well, same for journalists, then. There's only one difference: back then I was a journalist writing daily op-eds and now I'm a journalist writing daily specials!" Ali winked at Arif with one eye, his other eye following Omar who, after having sauntered off to buy something, returned hands full with a pineapple juice and a generous plate of food.

Kashif's mouth watered at the sight of the stuffed roti and fried plantain. He was tempted to get the same special but was trying to be careful with his money, now that he was starting to set his sights—really set his sights—on the police academy. Just being able to say the words, *becoming a cop*, had turned the seed of an idea into something that could actually take root. He had mentioned it to Zafar once, but that wasn't the same as talking to Frank, a *real-life* cop, who'd even praised him for his "good instincts" when he had struck up the nerve to say no one was taking the attack against that little mosque seriously enough.

Omar bit into the roti, its turmeric-stained sauce oozing out onto a Styrofoam plate, as Kashif's mind did somersaults trying to work out all the ways he could save up for the application fees and other costs he had read about on the OPP website. He had counted on most of his earnings going to help with their living expenses but, as it turned out, his mom was still getting financial support from his dad. He knew this because when he had tried to pay their rent the landlord said it had been taken care of already, "by his old man." He couldn't believe his mom would accept his dad's help! Had she no pride? But he remembered something his neighbours, the Osmans, were talking about in the elevator once: one of their cousins was getting divorced and they were debating how "nafaqa" would be observed. He didn't want to sound ignorant, so he googled it later and learned that it was a provision in Islam that entitled a wife to a husband's support in the event of separation. It sounded a lot like alimony—even if they were not officially divorced. At least this is what he understood of his parents' situation, and it had stopped him from doing something idiotic, like making his mom refuse his dad's money.

Kashif suppressed another stomach growl. It was the goat curry he was hankering after, because his mom rarely cooked goat even though she said it was a favourite in Pakistan. He consoled himself with the thought of the upcoming feast for Eid al-Adha, where the goat had a special significance as the symbol of Prophet Ibrahim's willingness to sacrifice his son.

Reminded of the festivities to come, Kashif managed to talk himself out of his craving, but everyone sat up hungrily when one of the kitchen staff appeared with a large tray filled with little golden balls and a dipping sauce.

"Pholouries for you boys!" Ali said, retrieving the rag from his shoulder. "No one leaves hungry at Al's! And you can't get to whatever serious business you've come to discuss on an empty stomach, right!"

Kashif thought the appetizers looked a lot like pakoras. When he bit into the little ball, he could detect a few of the usual ingredients— onions, cumin—but another bite revealed a different spectrum of tastes, including palette-scalding missiles of scotch bonnets that set his insides on fire.

"Enjoy!" Ali bowed theatrically and hummed his way back to the kitchen.

"Thank you, Uncle!" a chorus of mouths bulging with pholourie cried after him.

"And Kamal, I'm going to need you to help out soon," Ali called back for his son's benefit.

"OK," Nasser said, taking a breath, "We all know why we're here. Some of us were at Masjid Omar Bin Al-Hamad to help with the cleanup. And we all saw the hateful writing on the wall. We also know how it was handled. Only the most superficial police inquiry, which means we'll probably never know who did this. In a nutshell: no justice!"

They all nodded their agreement, except Jam who shot them a sneering glance.

Kashif wondered why this guy had come at all. He'd never hung out with Nasser before, and he didn't exactly fit the profile of Nasser's social circle, which mainly consisted of other business grads. He could only surmise the two of them had met at the Centre before his time— before he had become a fixture there.

"So, we're here because we all agree on something fundamental: we agree that the threat is still out there. And something needs to be done before," Nasser lowered his voice, "lives are lost, God forbid."

Kashif, who shared Nasser's sentiment, still felt compelled to point out the obvious: "But Ishaq-bhai doesn't seem to think that way. At least, he hasn't suggested that anyone's in any kind of danger."

"That's what he's saying to the public. But I know for a fact that isn't the case," Nasser leaned back and looked all around.

"How so?" Zafar asked flatly, prompting Jam to stop texting.

"Because I saw that letter for myself—the one Ishaq-bhai and the cops *aren't* talking about. And it's not the only one. That mosque has been on the receiving end of other threats. Even a death threat," Nasser said.

"So, what the hell did the letter say?" Jam pulled up his sleeves to reveal a large tattoo.

"Wow!" Arif ogled, pulling out his earbuds. "A snake!"

"Wrong!" Jam said coolly. "A dragon."

"Awesome!" Arif cooed.

Kashif could have sworn Jam flexed a bicep before repeating slowly, like he was talking to a room full of dimwits, "So . . . what did . . . the letter . . . say?"

"Look, first let's be clear that what I'm about to reveal to you all can never leave this room. I mean it!" Nasser asked his cousin to get him a drink and whispered, "No one is supposed to know about this. If it was, the police and Ishaq-bhai would have released it to the public. So, I need you all to swear that what I'm about to tell you stays between us . . . And remember: there is no greater sin in Islam than to take a false oath."

Kashif wasn't sure if that was the entire thrust of the hadith Nasser had referred to, but it had its desired effect.

"These letters are pretty much the same. They say things like, *Jihadis, get off our land!*" A groan of condemnation round the table seemed to satisfy Nasser. "*Your breeding grounds of terror are being watched.* And by that, he obviously means, any place where Muslims worship or gather."

"Only he?" Jam said, dropping the phone into his pocket. "How do you know it's only one guy? And why can't it be a woman?"

"Man, woman—doesn't matter! But the idiot slipped up a few times and said *I this* and *I that*. That's why the police think we're dealing with an amateur."

"I can just see the headlines now," Ismail waved a hand over his head. "*Lone Wolf Attacker Deemed Unfit to Stand Trial on Account of Mental Health Issues*! If that were a Muslim the whole world would be on red alert!"

"Preach!" Jam pushed his sleeve farther back to reveal a second tattoo comprised of Arabic script that Kashif immediately recognized as the Takbir, Allahu Akbar. God is great.

"It also said: *Action will be taken to stop this virus from spreading*," Nasser pressed on.

"Astaghfirullah!" Omar shuddered, folding his arms.

"There's more! The last part is why I called you guys here. It said: *Your Judgment Day awaits where you gather in the largest numbers, and on your most sacred days*."

Ismail released a louder whistle. "That's heavy."

"It's a direct threat, that's what it is!" Nasser gesticulated, the glint of his gold watch blinding Kashif for a split second.

"Why didn't the police reveal all this? And why didn't Ishaq-bhai push for a proper investigation?" Omar verbalized Kashif's silent deliberations.

"The point is they don't want the community in a state of panic," Zafar said. "Because creating panic and terror is what it's all about. I read about this kind of thing when the #Punish-a-Muslim campaign was investigated in England."

"I heard about that," Omar said. "It was like a Pokeyman game, only points were given for doing things like pulling off hijabs, or insulting a Muslim in public, or much, much worse, like nuking Mecca or using Abu Ghraib-style torture tactics."

"Yeah, but in England those threats went all the way to some pretty high-profile people, including some white politicians sympathetic to their Muslim supporters. If not, the police probably wouldn't have taken it as seriously as they did. They even launched a counter-terrorism squad to investigate it."

"Well, that's just my point! We don't have CSIS much less MI5 running interference for us," Nasser interjected, "but I do have it on good intel that—"

"That the little mosque was just a test run." Ismail's face darkened.

"Exactly!" Nasser seized on the analogy. "And with Eid festivities just around the corner, the Centre's the obvious choice for a *large gathering*, like the one hinted at in the letter."

Ismail's face expanded again: "And Eid al-Adha will be really well attended. It's the big Eid, after all."

"And this year Thanksgiving is just before Eid," Omar noted.

"So?" Nasser said, kneading his temple.

"Just thought I'd mention it," Omar shrugged, making everyone snort.

"Look, this is no joke!" Nasser started as a young woman wearing yoga pants and a body-hugging t-shirt came and whispered something in Kamal's ear. As she sashayed away Kashif caught her smiling at Jam.

"My sister, Farida." Kamal said self-consciously. "We've got deliveries I have to help out with."

"Yeah, for the love of God, speed it up!" Jam said, his eyes fixed on Kamal's sister.

Nasser leaned in. "Look, there is a slim chance that Ishaq-bhai will hire a private security detail to guard the entrance during the peak hours of the Eid dinner, and he said something about a new security system—alarms, cameras, that sort of stuff—but it won't be installed before Eid."

"It sounds like he's on top of it, then," Kashif said.

"It's *something* but it's not nearly enough. It's a huge facility with several side exits and entrances that someone could slip into and out of without looking suspicious. And Kamal just reminded me that people will be making deliveries all day long."

Kashif was as impressed by Nasser's attention to detail as he was surprised by his obvious devotion to the cause. He always chalked him up to being a bit smug, with his bling-y watch and his stuffy suits. But then again, he reckoned he was just biased because of his dad's stories about what jerks some of those bank manager-types were, treating him like scum when he was looking for a job.

"So, here's the plan," Nasser resumed. "We're going to take shifts and watch the building. *We* are going to be the round-the-clock surveillance, inside and outside. Think of it as a Neighbourhood Watch. That's a very Canadian thing, right!"

"Not just Canadian—some Muslim communities have formed permanent Neighbourhood Watches in New York. I know, because my cousin there is part of one," Ismail said. "It seems to work quite well."

"There we go! We'll be like our American brothers!"

"OK, so what are we supposed to do on this surveillance—I mean, on this Neighbourhood Watch?" Zafar asked.

"We'll position ourselves around parts of the building at different times to keep an eye out for anything, or *anyone*, suspicious. Ishaq-bhai will have a list of people authorized to come in and out of the building before and after the festivities start. I'll make sure I get a copy."

"Ishaq-bhai's in the loop, then?"

"Of course not, Zafar! He'd never concede to this."

"But what if we see something or *someone*?" Omar ventured. "What do we do, then?"

"Whatever it takes."

"What if he's armed? What if he's got a bomb!" Kashif's mind raced through the possible extremes. "I mean, if a terrorist is planning an attack, then don't we have to be ready for . . . anything?"

"Someone's got to step up here!" Nasser raised his voice and then lowered it when a set of diners glared at them.

Then Jam, of all people, asked the million-dollar question: "So what are you going to do if you catch the creep—or creeps?"

"We're the first line of defense," Nasser said. "We'll do what we have to."

"You guys are such amateurs!" Jam pushed back his chair "I'm out!"

"Hey, this isn't a *Dragon's Den* episode! You can't just say *I'm out!*" Nasser lost his cool. "You're part of this now, Jam! We took the oath!"

"Then call me when you grow a pair!" Jam goaded, though his focus was on the Staff Only door, which Farida had pushed open just enough for him to take notice and give her a flirtatious wink on his way out.

No one said a word, conscious of the extent to which Nasser's pride had taken a hit.

"Is Jam a gangster?" Arif asked, returning with another ginger beer.

"Actually, I was thinking the same thing," Ismail said. "That dragon image: isn't it the symbol of one of those Asian gangs?"

"First, that's racist, man! And second, I don't know what's up with those tattoos. He probably just thinks they make him look hot or something!" Nasser said and fell back into his chair.

"I heard he has a police record," Omar said.

"What did he do?" Kashif asked.

"He hooked up with some youth gang that held up convenience stores," Omar said.

"Did he serve time?"

"He was only fifteen. I guess he should have faced some jail time back then, as a juvie. But the point is," Nasser regained some of his bluster, "his dad's a big shot. You know who one of the biggest donors at the Centre is, right?"

Ismail whistled, impressed. "You mean his dad is *that* Mr Maker? The guy who coughed up the money for the pool and the athletic facilities?"

"Oh, he's way more than a donor!" Kamal interjected with a tinge of sarcasm. "He practically bankrolled that place! And it's the biggest Islamic Cultural Centre in the country. Maybe across North America, even!"

"Like I said, he's loaded, so he lawyered up to get Jam's sentence reduced to community service." Nasser rubbed his watch strap, which had worn down in parts, revealing its fake gold plating. "And he convinced Ishaq-bhai to let him do his time at the Centre."

"But that was years ago, right?" Zafar observed. "I've never seen him around. Not as a volunteer, not at namaaz, or anything else."

"Look, I don't know what's in it for him. Maybe he wants to pay it forward!"

"Kamal!" Kamal's dad tried to get his son's attention.

"Well, I am assuming you're all in, then!" Nasser said, signalling the meeting officially adjourned.

Omar dove into the roti he had set aside, and Kashif decided he might as well stay for a late lunch. He searched the menu for goat curry roti specials when Nasser walked up to him: "And that cop friend of yours better not get wind of this."

Cop? Kashif spun around but Nasser was already out the door. Which cop? Frank? But how on earth could Nasser know he had met some random cop! Then paranoia set in: maybe Frank wasn't a cancer patient, like his mom. Maybe he was one of those CSIS guys planted to spy on them . . . But why? *They* hadn't done anything wrong! They were just volunteers at the Centre! They were just trying to help out! There was no crime in that!

8

Arubah had come this close to foregoing the Tariq al-Nur meeting. It wasn't really a meeting, after all. Dr Ali asked the women to help prepare informational mail-out packages. But the campaign alerted her to so many new ways of approaching domestic violence and women's rights in Islam, like its intercultural and gender-inclusive therapies, that she had come to see it as a complement to many of her academic courses.

And there was Kashif, most likely still sitting in the lobby. Part of her was mortified. Had she really just spilled her guts out to this guy? The other part wished she hadn't pushed the "close door" button on the elevator. A weight had instantly lifted off her shoulders after she'd told him what had happened. What if he hadn't been there? Why was she so convinced Marisol wouldn't be as sympathetic as Kashif—a guy? She knew why. She just didn't want to admit it. She just assumed Marisol would be the type to say *I told you so.* She didn't want to be made to feel like this was the price she had to pay for wearing a hijab, bringing attention to herself. Like it was *her* fault! . . .

And yet, there was more to it than that. When Kashif was sitting less than an arm's-length away from her on the bench, she had wanted to grab his hand. She could have put her head on his shoulders and stayed there forever. She hadn't felt that way about a guy since her schoolgirl crush on Rob Miller, the teacher's pet, in seventh grade. Perhaps it was just a case of frayed nerves. She couldn't possibly be thinking straight—not after that horrible incident. Whatever she was feeling, it was all in her head. Attraction. Chemistry. These were just silly, idle, foolish thoughts. Impure thoughts, some of the more conservative women in the room might say. Haram.

None of the women seemed to notice Arubah's lateness when she entered the boardroom they had taken over for the day, and she was immediately put to work, sorting through a stack of brochures, which had been translated into several languages, courtesy of Tasneem Baksh, an object of much admiration among this group. The brochures would be mailed out to Islamic associations across the country.

It was a relief to concentrate on a mindless task—until the idle chit-chat turned to more serious subjects. Some of it concerned the attack on a Rexdale mosque not all that far from where she and her mom lived, and there was some hushed debate about whether the imam could have pushed for a more in-depth investigation. But some of the women were ardent defenders of Ishaq-bhai's approach, arguing that a police investigation would only be *for show*. The general perception seemed to be that the police only intervened in the worst-case scenarios—*blood* had to be spilled before anyone took notice.

"Anyway, what have the police ever done for us?" a woman named Uzma said, as she emptied out a box of lapel pins with "Tariq al-Nur" embossed over a Crescent Moon.

Another woman, who was from Sudan, added, "Once I go police. Our Honda-car stolen. But I no speak good English and could not fill form."

"And why are there are no female officers?" a woman in niqab said indignantly. "Always men, men, men! It makes it too hard to talk to the police. If there's any problem now, I phone my friends or I come here! What else to do?"

"But it's even harder when it's one of us who's attacked for the way we look," a younger woman in hijab spoke up. "Maybe they think we're just being hysterical or something. So now I just fight my own battles!"

"Yes, beti," Uzma agreed. "My daughter Sehr says the same thing. So many times, she's been insulted or bullied because of her hijab, so now she just tells me, 'Mom, it happens all the time. I don't want to talk about it!' "

Arubah always took issue with adolescent girls wearing hijab, a practice she figured only cloistered old men could endorse from the safety of their minarets and ivory towers, far removed from the kind of schoolyard bullying Sehr obviously faced on a daily basis. And she felt a little ashamed at the thought of someone as young as Sehr fighting her own battles when she, herself, had felt so helpless around those teenagers. It was the shock of it. Having her hijab ripped from her! Something so close to her body it was like a second skin. It was odd to think of it this way, considering that she only made the decision to wear hijab after high school, right before her freshman year at uni. But she had always admired the women who adopted it despite the backlash and judgment it aroused, sometimes even from other Muslims who supported the head-covering bans. For her, it was a reminder to hold fast to everything she believed in, especially when her more compassionate side was tested by a menacing glance or a spiteful comment, or when her more charitable side was subdued by her own preoccupations and desires. She had grown up around too many kids who were embarrassed or insecure about something or the other: their colour, their weight, the material things they did or didn't have . . . There was always something. When she first veiled herself, it wasn't as if her own insecurities fell away. It was more about what she gained. The strength and courage to live in her body as she chose.

Arubah touched her ear, the violent grip of that girl from the bus still fresh enough to sting. There was a sticky deposit, like a spot of blood, on her earlobe, and she was about to excuse herself for a quick washroom break, but someone had started to speak with a calming, measured voice.

"Uzma-bhain, I am truly sorry Sehr has had to endure so much. This is why we're trying to create alternative spaces for our sisters to talk about their experiences. I hope Sehr knows she can come to me and the other Counsellors whenever she needs."

"It's good to know that you're here for us, Dr Ali," a pregnant woman handing out rounds of tea said and set down her tray, "but when these things are happening you are not out there with us. We're on our own. And that's when we have to react. In my case, if I get spit at, I spit back. If I am told *fuck-this* and *fuck-that*, I'll just say *fuck-this* and *fuck-that* right back! Seeing such an 'oppressed woman' cursing in their language usually shocks them into silence! I know it's haram to say such things but if it's the only weapon I have to defend myself then, as God is my witness, I'll use it!"

Some of the women laughed shyly, but Arubah also detected more than a few looks of recrimination before an elderly woman called Rifat-begum took it upon herself to speak up: "You mustn't do this! It gives Islam a bad name. You're attracting too much negative attention!"

The woman next to her stood up: "Rifat-begum is right! We are all ambassadors here! It is our role to represent Islam. We have to be above reproach! Aren't we all sinners who behave as sinners!" She stood as stiff and erect as her heavily pleated sari when she realized she had the room's attention. "We are not just letting ourselves down! We are letting our brothers and sisters down! We are defiling the name of our Prophet—May Peace Be Upon Him!"

"Salla Allahu Alayhi Wasallum!" Rifat-begum said a prayer in veneration of the Prophet Muhammad, and everyone returned to the task at hand.

Arubah continued to organize the translated brochures into their respective piles—English, French, Urdu, Bengali, Arabic—when Uzma whispered that someone was waiting for her outside. Arubah got up in surprise and went into the hall, where a kid she recognized from one of the youth programs was holding out his hand, a gold circle nestled in his palm.

"My earring!" Arubah took the ring from his hand. "But how did you find it! And how on earth did you know it's mine!"

"Kashif-bhai found it."

"Kashif? . . . But how? When!"

"I don't know. He had to go somewhere so he asked me to give it to you!"

"Wow! I mean, thanks!" Arubah wasted no time in putting the earring back on, and then touched it in disbelief. Had Kashif really gone to such lengths to find it for her?

She ducked back into the boardroom, where the heaviness of recent discussions had yielded to more lighthearted chatter, like how much to budget for children's Eid gifts these days, and the best place to get a shalwar kameez tailored, for Eid night.

9

Frank rang the doorbell a second time: "Chris, where the hell are you?" He had a key but he hesitated to use it without Cheryl's permission. He had done that enough times to know it only made things worse, and he sure as hell didn't want to walk in on his ex-wife and *the Suit*.

He rang again while casually surveying their old Etobicoke neighbourhood; his apartment was not far. Too close for comfort, according to Cheryl, but that didn't stop her from treating him like the local handyman before the Suit came on the scene. No wonder the house looked as bad as it did: everything from the door frame to the roof shingles to the maple tree could have used some TLC. Why Cheryl didn't give Chris some responsibility was beyond him. It was time he started earning his keep.

Frank held down the doorbell, something he'd never have done if there was any chance Cheryl were home. He had been trying to get hold of Chris for days, to tell him the good news about the remission. Something wasn't right, he thought anxiously. It was one thing for Chris to mope around the house in his jammies all day playing video games, but another thing to be completely MIA.

Frank slipped behind a browning cedar and peered into the window but the curtains were drawn. He hated Cheryl's habit of keeping the drapes closed to protect the upholstery. It was a piece of furniture, for crying out loud! It was meant to see daylight! Why did she insist on making their house look like a morgue!

Deep down he blamed himself for these blackout conditions. What had that counsellor said? "Sometimes control is displaced from relationships to objects." That was the last time they had gone to see her but the message had stuck. Now he wondered if he'd made a mistake. Would it have killed him to sit through a few more sessions?

"Chris!" Frank rapped on the window before walking back to the porch and phoning Cheryl.

"Hello?"

"Frank?" a hollow voice replied over the voices and alarms of an overcrowded emergency ward. "You know I'm at work, right?"

"I'm sorry, I'm just looking for Chris."

"Why? Has something happened?"

"I thought *you* could tell me that! He's not answering my calls!"

"Well, I haven't seen him in a few days. Maybe a week."

"A few days or a week, which is it?"

"He's twenty-four years old. He does his own thing. I don't watch his every move. That's his old man's MO!"

Frank held the phone away from his ear to compose himself. "I just want to know where he is! Give me something I can work with, Cheryl!"

"Frank, I don't have time for this!"

"OK, OK! I have some news. It's important . . . I'm in full remission!"

"Really?"

"Well, don't crack open the champagne on my account!"

Frank pictured his ex-wife at the other end, her hair held together in a scrunchy, in her pale-blue scrubs and the white sneakers which she used to kick off the minute she got home. She was tired then like she sounded tired now. She was always tired. Too tired to talk. Too tired to go on vacations. Too tired for sex. Too tired to see the walls closing in on them . . .

"Considering the good news, and what with Thanksgiving coming up and all, I wondered if maybe . . . we could celebrate. The three of us."

Frank heard buzzers and someone wailing in the background.

"Can this wait?"

"Well, you've been a big help, I must say!" Frank felt the sting of her rebuff.

"Look, I know you're at the house, so just let yourself in!"

"How—"

"Twenty-five years with a cop rubs off on you, I guess."

Frank winced over the twenty-five-year milestone they'd never got to celebrate because Cheryl had asked him to move out a few weeks shy of their anniversary, the silver heart-shaped locket he'd bought her still sitting at the bottom of his sock drawer. "But what about the Suit—I mean, Bill?"

"That's over." Cheryl didn't give Frank the time to respond. "And Frank, I'm sorry, I didn't mean to shrug off your news about the remission. It's amazing. It really is."

"Yeah . . . thanks." Frank let her hang up first. He sat on the porch step and rubbed his chest. His conversations with Cheryl, however superficial, however brief, always left him winded. And had she really just said she and Bill were done? If Chris were around, he could give him the backstory of why things went south.

Frank pored through his text messages again. Nothing. Not a single message. He scrolled through his call history. Nothing.

An elderly man with a cane walked by. He was dressed in the long shirt that Frank had seen some of the Muslim men wearing. It was long enough to be sticking out under a parka. The man noticed Frank sitting on the porch step and tipped his head in acknowledgement.

Frank returned the gesture, thinking about his conversations outside that building—the vandalized mosque. He had only intended to check things out from his car, curious whether this was, in fact, the same place that was on the news. He and Wade had dealt with this kind of thing before. Once they were called out to a break-in at a synagogue—there was little missing or vandalized so it became more of an insurance matter than a police matter. He figured he wouldn't have given this incident too much thought either, if it weren't for that young man at the hospital. He'd seemed pretty level-headed—like he had good instincts.

Frank had always hoped his son would follow in his footsteps, but the little-boy thrill of riding in cop cars and being allowed to play with the siren wore off by the time Chris got his first gaming console. Even if he were to show some interest in it now, Frank had to wonder what kind of shape he'd be in. He wouldn't survive the first five minutes of the physical endurance tests. And he had zero respect for authority— at least if the tone he took with the MWGHL were any indication.

This guy, Kar-shift, on the other hand. He was a different story. Frank felt he had a sixth sense for these things, having also had the task of mentoring many of the rookies at the Sixth Division. Just the fact that he'd been looking out for his mom when most guys his age would be running wild—like his own son, no doubt—was already a good mark of character. Besides all that, he liked the kid's spirit of volunteerism. Church, mosque, the YMCA. Did it make any difference in the end, so long as these kids were taught to care about something other than themselves?

A young woman walked by the house pushing a stroller. She had a different kind of scarf over her head. It reminded him of the mosque again. Why he felt the need to take a closer look was beyond him. Even if he were back on duty he would have no jurisdiction there, but a fresh set of eyes never hurt. And could anyone blame him for needing to feel like a cop again? For wanting his life to amount to more than a good day or a bad day on chemo.

"Did Mr Khan send you back here?"

"I'm sorry?" Frank looked up to meet a congenial face under an unusually broad camel-coloured hat.

"Ishaq Khan, the Director of the Islamic Cultural Centre?" the man clarified.

"Uh no! I'm here on my own," Frank said vaguely, dubbing camel-hat-man, CHM, like Chum.

Chum was joined by an elderly bearded fellow, and they proceeded to exchange words in a language which sounded like the one spoken by Kay-chef's mother, at least the little he'd overheard at the hospital. The older man gave him a once-over and went back inside. This seemed to incite some curiosity from within, and a younger man in business attire and a few gold accessories came to join them. The get-up reminded Frank too much of Bill, so Frank nicknamed him SOS, for the Slick-Other-Suit.

"The police were already here this morning," SOS said.

"I imagine so."

"So, how did you hear about what happened?"

"Oh, it was on the local news, but I was also talking to a young man about it. One of your volunteers . . . Kar-shift or Kay-chef, I think."

"Kashif? Kashif Siddiqui?"

"I'm sorry, I'm terrible with names as it is, and my pronunciation is the worst!"

"So, you *are* a cop, then?" SOS persisted, too brashly for Frank's liking.

There was some yelling from inside the building. Frank could hear a woman's voice answer back. He was about to leave before he was the one subject to an interrogation, but Chum motioned for him to stay. "Please, we're bringing you chai."

"Excuse me?" Frank wiped away a few beads of sweat. He didn't know why the encounter was making him so jittery. Was he so out of practice?

"A cup of tea!" SOS said, as if Frank were hard of hearing.

"Oh, chai-tea, yes, it's all the rage, isn't it!" Frank eased up.

"Not *that* chai! This is *real* chai. Homemade!" the older man wagged his finger on his return.

"Ah, of course, but really, you needn't trouble—"

"No, please!" Chum smiled. "We are providing food and

refreshments for anyone who drops in today. In appreciation for community support."

Frank was had. He couldn't refuse their *appreciation*! He was about to say as much when a woman with a long black braid appeared with two Styrofoam cups. She was wearing a billowy tunic, much like the two older men, only hers was brightly patterned, and she had a long scarf loosely draped over her head. She handed the two cups to the older man, who proceeded to pass one over to Frank and keep the second one for himself.

The tea smelled so fragrant, the heat it generated a much-needed antidote to the nip in the air. Frank took a sip, realizing it was the first thing he'd consumed since the Danish he'd purchased from the hospital cafeteria. "This is very nice, thank you."

Chum received a call, so Frank took the opportunity to do a quick once-over of the building. The glass from the broken windows had been cleared up, with MDF boards put in the place of missing windows, and the writing on the wall was scrubbed clean and painted over, except for a few missed spots on the side wall.

"WCF," Frank read aloud.

"Yeah. No one knows what that means." SOS shadowed Frank. "But that reporter suggested it might mean *White Canada Forever*—some old propaganda line from back in the day."

"And this other one: FAIR. What's that about?" Frank touched the wall, moving his finger along indentations chiselled into the brick.

"Beats me! The imam here said he's had to paint over graffiti like this plenty of times, but he's never seen that one before. He said he only noticed it this morning, after the attack."

"Hmmm." Frank had to agree that FAIR stood out. "So, did this acronym appear in the letter they were talking about on the news?"

"Your guess is as good as mine," SOS shrugged, but Frank sensed he knew more than he was letting on.

"The police—your people—will do what they can," the elder man stepped in.

"Sure they will!" SOS crossed his arms.

"That's a great hat, by the way." Frank said when Chum rejoined them, sensing he may have out-stayed his welcome.

"Thank you," Chum smiled. "It is a chitrali cap."

"Right! Well, it's splendid!" Frank emptied out the last drop of chai, before hastening back to his car.

———

"Chris!" Frank used his fist to knock on the door this time. Even though Cheryl had given him permission to let himself in, he felt like a trespasser in a place that had erased all trace of his existence, except for the odd family photo and the furniture Cheryl had claimed in the divorce.

He unlocked the door, half expecting the key not to work. He could never tell with Cheryl. He was even more surprised that she had suggested he let himself in. He must have given her the impression that he was really panicked about Chris. But he was embarrassed to admit that he hadn't dwelt too much on Chris lately, having been far too pre-occupied by the prognosis he'd been waiting for. It was only on hearing the good news that it had dawned on him just how long it had been since he had spoken to his son.

"I'm sure that boy's just holed up in the basement," he muttered as he entered a sun-deprived house. He bumped his shin on the coffee table, cursing as he pulled open the drapes. Could Chris be so far out of touch that he hadn't even noticed how dark it was inside?

"Chris! It's Dad!" he called out irritably, before heading for the basement, which Chris had turned into his own private suite.

"Chris!" he yelled from the top of the stairs. The basement was as dark as the main floor, so Frank turned on the light and headed down, half expecting to find a snoring twenty-something curled up in bed with a hangover.

"Chris?" he tried again, as he got to the bottom of the stairs. The bed was unmade but there was nothing unusual to note in that. Everything looked like the room of his vagabond-son.

Frank rifled through Chris's video game collection stacked in a corner next to a pile of technical bits and bobs that he assumed had to do with Chris's computer. It made him think to look for Chris's laptop, which he rarely left home without. Coming up empty, Frank felt something in the pit of his stomach, but he couldn't tell if it was a cop's hunch or a father's sixth sense. He did another scan of the room before heading back upstairs. Once at the top he had a change of heart and went back down. This time he decided to dig deeper, almost falling back when a large poster started to peel off a closet door.

"Free Farms of 160 Acres. Dominion of Canada," he read the captions in a map showing a migration path from Europe to Canada. The old poster seemed harmless enough so he pushed the corner back over the double-sided tape. It dropped back down, just enough to reveal the right angles of a letter etched into the melamine surface. Frank rubbed his finger over it, gauging the depth of the indentation was made with the Swiss Army knife he'd gifted his son when they still went camping together. Frank teased the poster edge back a bit more, careful not to tear it, when he was interrupted by a call. He stopped to check if it was Chris, ready to chew him out for vandalizing the furniture, but an unfamiliar number appeared on the screen.

"Hello," Frank answered. "Oh, Kar-shift! Yes, of course I remember you!"

Frank shut the closet door and made his way back upstairs.

"Sure, I'd be happy to meet up," he said, oblivious to the poster dropping to the floor. "How about this Thanksgiving weekend?"

10

Kashif was back home in bed but he couldn't fall asleep—not after that meeting with Nasser and the guys, all kinds of thoughts running through his head. He turned on his bedside light, sat up, and picked up the book on the nightstand. It was one of his dad's old favourites, *The Great Indus Journey*. It seemed a bit dry but as he flipped through the pages, he became absorbed. The book was peppered with maps. One of them showed the trajectory of the Indus from what was described as the "roof of the world," at the Himalayan summit, right down to the southern tip of Pakistan. The great river "ebbed and flowed like an aortic cavity," the author wrote, pumping the lands with glacial waters that few would identify as such by the time they reached the desert plains surrounding Karachi. Kashif studied the map of Karachi, his parents' city of birth, where the Indus concluded its journey. The branches of the Indus Delta looked like little arms reaching out to the Arabian Sea. If you turned the map upside down, it appeared as if the sea's open arms had invited the river in. But whichever way you looked at it, the river seemed to vanish at this point. He flipped through another set of maps, settling on a satellite image showing how the Indus had carved a canyon in the seabed, where it had deposited layers of sediment accumulated along its journey. From this perspective, the river seemed to get stronger by merging with the sea, adding new layers to its submarine floor, changing the sea's identity, granule by granule.

Kashif paused, considering the other aspect of the river—its glacial origins. He had never really thought of "glacial" and "Pakistan" in the same sentence. Seeing the Indus start its life in snow-covered mountains, where it ran as clear and cold as any Canadian river, made the place seem less desolate, less foreign. It enticed him to crack open the first chapter. Apparently, there were some pretty important archaeological sites along the Indus, like the ancient cities of Harappa and Mohenjodaro, which had grown along the riverbanks over four thousand years ago. The author called them one of the oldest civilizations on record, with advanced agricultural technology and urban planning. In school he had never learned anything about Pakistan. India had come up once with the stock image of the Taj Mahal, which was treated like a national landmark. The Mughal emperor who built it didn't come up at all, much less the question of which landmark rightfully belonged to which country after Partition—a subject that always made a vein bust out of his dad's temple.

Kashif read through a full chapter, eager to find out about the Pakistan his parents knew and loved—not just the ancient side of things but the cities they had grown up in. But contemporary Pakistan didn't get much coverage, and when it did, it didn't sound like a place worth visiting. It was almost as if the cities of Harappa and Mohenjodaro were one-offs in a backward place—relics of an ancient past that had little to do with the present. He was reminded of that Indiana Jones film—the one with the crystal skulls, where aliens seemed the more plausible builders of an advanced civilization than the Indigenous people who had lived there for millennia.

Kashif closed the book and lay on his side, frustrated by the author's comment that the Arabian Sea was the only solace in a "city of extremes." She may as well have said *extremists*, Kashif burned—but why was he getting so defensive about a place he knew so little about? All he had to go on were his parents' photos which, with a few small exceptions, were mainly selfies taken in relatives' homes or at big weddings. And if he could have such a narrow view of a place to which he was connected, if not by birth, then at least by all those other meta-things like family, culture, religion, then what would it look like to those with absolutely no such connections?

Why couldn't community elders like Ishaq-bhai see this? Couldn't they see they wore a distorted target on their backs, making them ripe for suspicion and attack? And why did they feel they had to play down what happened at the mosque? Did they have to accept prejudice as the price to pay for living here, like an undisclosed immigration fee? Whichever way he spun it, the only sensible thing to do always went back to calling the police and letting them do their job. They would look at the mosque attack more objectively, and with those letters that Nasser had spoken of, they would have something to work with. Something concrete to build a case on. But then again, that could take years, and it wouldn't guarantee their safety on Eid night, which was fast-approaching.

Kashif rolled over and buried his face in his pillow. He didn't want to admit it, but in spite of his thousand and one doubts, he couldn't see himself backing out now from the resolve of that meeting. That would mean bailing out on his friends. His bhaiyas, his brothers, from the Centre.

At first, volunteering at the Centre and even signing up for the odd Quranic lesson, had given him a much-needed change of scenery. He even thought he could convince his mom to check out the place. She was the one who really needed to get out of the house. Her whole world revolved around those treatments, the hospital, the medications, her illness. She needed to talk to people. To other women like her. She could even get involved in things, like that campaign, Tariq al-Nur; the kinds of activities the Princess Margaret offered didn't seem to appeal to her one bit. Maybe she would get drawn back into attending juma and other religious services. She used to do namaaz at home, at least before the cancer had sapped her strength. More recently, he had resorted to leaving the Centre's brochures lying around the apartment on the off-chance she'd notice them. Just the other day he'd seen her looking over the pamphlets on the coffee table, and she didn't immediately toss them out, but then that stupid bird had distracted her. She loved feeding those damn birds even though all they ever did was take a dump on the balcony.

Now he was the one who'd become a permanent fixture at the Centre. As far as the religious stuff went, he was still trying to figure things out. He loved doing namaaz, though he wasn't great at it. Sometimes he'd turn his face left when others were turning their face right. Or he would rise up too soon, or sit down too fast. And he only performed namaaz at juma. It hadn't become a daily practice. He didn't want his mom to think he was trying to send her a message. He was convinced she'd take it all wrong, like he'd turned to God to absolve them of something *she'd* done! Sometimes he got the impression that she blamed everything on herself—the cancer, his dad abandoning them, maybe even for leaving Pakistan behind, though coming here was his dad's dream, not hers. This made his dad's betrayal even greater. His mom should have been surrounded by her family at a time like this, and yet here she was, dealing with cancer entirely on her own—well, not entirely alone. He did what he could to support her, but that was hardly the same as his dad being here. He could forgive his dad a lot of things, but abandoning his poor mom when she could be dying! He never said it out loud but he knew it was in the realm of possibility.

Thank God for the Centre, Kashif thought. And for Ishaq-bhai. He may have been disappointed by the imam's response to the attack, but Ishaq-bhai never treated him like some of those high-and-mighty maulana-types his dad railed against for taking Islam back to the Stone Age. "And they're not even coming from a Muslim country! They're coming from Nottingham and Liverpool, for God's sake, with their British accents on the one hand, and their bigotry and intolerance on the other!"

If it weren't for Ishaq-bhai, Kashif knew he wouldn't have stuck around the Centre for this long. Ishaq-bhai had immediately picked up on his depression and set him up as a volunteer. First, it was just the odd job here or there. Then, he appointed him as a kind of big brother for the new youth program at the Centre. It was mainly directed at troubled youth but also served as a childcare service to those in need. Kashif started looking forward to helping the kids. They could be really goofy, like Nasser's cousin, and it got him to ease up and laugh a little, too. It was the first thing he'd done in his life that seemed to make sense—something that made him realize he wanted more out of life than just a paycheque. He wanted to make a difference.

He thought about the upcoming Eid celebration at the Centre. There would be hundreds of people there, including kids and all the people he knew. He wondered if his mom was planning on attending. He wished she would, but then again, what if there was some sort of attack on Eid night? And Arubah? He hoped she'd be at the Eid dinner, though now he couldn't stomach the thought of her or anyone else being in danger. He realized he was bending towards Nasser's way of thinking.

Kashif turned on his back and looked up at the watermark on the ceiling. It had been there for as long as he could remember. It used to drive him nuts but now in its permanence it was strangely comforting. Perhaps things would go back to normal.

Kashif took a deep breath. He missed talking to his dad. He may have been short on time but never on opinions. These all had to do with the news and world politics, but Kashif hated how silent the apartment was without him, especially with his mom so weak and unreachable. He even missed the way his dad used to borrow his laptop to read the international news. Sometimes Kashif would find a piece in Reuters or Al Jazeera left up on the screen, forcing him to peer into parts of the world—South Asia, the Middle East, Iran—that had never held too much interest for him, at least until now. He'd done more reading in the past year, poring through his dad's old books, than in all his high school years combined. At least it felt that way, if only because things were so black-and-white in high school, where the subjects were as neatly compartmentalized as the students: biology, language, English, math, geek, nerd, jock, . . . A few of his old friends were in cool-sounding college programs now, like Digital Gaming or Industrial Robotics. It had almost motivated him to apply, but to what end? What was the point of racking up a lifetime of student debt just to say he had a degree? He knew his parents were disappointed in him, but he was grateful they hadn't pushed too hard. On the other hand, he wished they knew more about the system here; neither had gone to university. His dad had completed some admin program in Pakistan but it didn't count for much here. Kashif didn't want to be in the same boat. He wanted to do something that counted.

Kashif heard a TV come on in the apartment above them. The walls were thin enough to make out the weather announcer droning on about the week ahead. Snow would come early this year, he remembered hearing before turning in, a habit of watching the news before bed, like his dad. He always did a drum roll in his head, anticipating his dad's favourite mantra, "No news is *not* good news, you understand! News is always worthwhile. Take the people back home, from the most illiterate to the most educated, from the poorest to the richest—they all keep themselves informed about the world they live in. You know why that is?" He'd turn to Kashif who'd invariably kick himself for not changing the channel. "Because those who live under the shadow of power know that the only light in their path is information. Information is survival, you understand?"

Kashif would nod at this point, desperate to get back to his Reality TV shows, but this only set his dad off again.

"Though this bloody local news is something else! They treat us like brainless twits, with more feel-good stories about dogs and squirrels than anything real—anything hard-hitting!"

It occurred to Kashif that his dad might not have been aware of the mosque attack, since he didn't always make a point of watching the "bloody local news." If the press were informed about the contents of that letter and all the others like it, then maybe, just maybe it would have been worth some attention! Maybe it could even have made the international news.

He wished he could tell his dad about the attack, the hateful messages painted on the walls of that mosque. *Terrorists. Illegals. Go home.* Law-abiding Muslims were being terrorized and yet it was *they* who were labeled the terrorists—people who had come here with Canada's blessing, no less. And if this place wasn't home for someone like him, born at the Toronto General, then what was? He'd never set foot in Pakistan! Where was he supposed to go!

Kashif picked up the book and resumed reading: "From the time of the Indus cities, until the advent of trains in the nineteenth century, the river was the spinal cord of all local trade, connecting towns and villages, resources and people that otherwise would never have met."

"People that otherwise would never have met," he read the line again, his mind circling back to his own chance meeting with Frank. With Arubah. With all the people whose lives were becoming tangled up with his own.

But how did Nasser know about Frank? Where would *they* have met?

II

Defense of Provocation

11

Arubah watched the landscape between Toronto and Montreal roll by like a commercial on mute. Once the train passed the industrial sprawl east of Toronto, there was nothing to see but undulating farms. Here and there the view was punctuated by a cluster of trees, which either stood in naked silhouettes or added hits of colour to a flat grey sky.

The train was filled to capacity with university students heading back home for Thanksgiving weekend. Arubah found herself stealing glances at a couple wearing matching university sweatshirts, their lips locked in a deep wet kiss till one of them looked up and she turned back to her book, flushed with embarrassment.

Marisol had fallen asleep almost as soon as the train pulled out of Union Station, leaving Arubah with little to distract her. She leafed through the post-it notes marking the chapters she was supposed to review for midterms, her thoughts drifting to that last lecture in Gender and Social Justice. She fished out her course reader where she had highlighted the prof's comment about the most "horrific honour killing ever to be carried out on Canadian soil." In truth, all she really wanted to do at present was to talk to Marisol. They hadn't seen each other since that lecture, and she'd been saving up all her news for the train. Where would she start: with the good stuff about Kashif, or with her ordeal outside the Centre?

She still had a hard time understanding what had happened that day. Did the teens retaliate because she stuck up for that poor woman and her child on the bus? Surely what they were doing was more dangerous than a bit of immature heckling? So why did she feel so uncomfortable putting *teenagers* and *hate crime* in the same sentence? Could they really feel such hatred so young? She had read about the high rates of teen bullying directed at marginalized groups in her Sociology course. It was the same scale of prejudice and ignorance, only played out among a younger demographic. Had she become a statistic now? A case study for a sociology class? How would *she* be classified in a student's term paper? *Female Victim of Racialized Teen Bullying*. What if she were a news headline? *Anti-Muslim Attack Victim Speaks Out in Greater Toronto Area*. Maybe she wouldn't even factor into a scholarly essay: *Escalating Hate Crimes and Incidents of Islamophobia Among Late Adolescents*.

Arubah doodled on the front page of the course reader, wondering if she should hold off telling Marisol what had happened to her. This was supposed to be a fun trip—a break from the heavy stuff. And Marisol had a tendency to get heated up about everything and she'd definitely *lose her shit*, as she liked to say. Marisol was all "action and adventure," whereas Arubah thought of herself as one of the more newfangled TV genres, like a "procedural drama." Was it wrong to take time to process things, to sort through the data coming at her, before voicing an opinion or taking up arms? In the classroom, it was the vocal types who were immediately rewarded, though at least Marisol always had something intelligent to say. She would never raise a hand for the sake of it; she would never speak just to call attention to herself.

Arubah looked at the letter "K" she had doodled on the course reader. Who was acting like a teenager now! She had three midterms to study for, not to mention the final paper for Professor March's course. The assignment required a critical analysis of one of their case studies, and she had planned to look over her notes on the "honour killings" case. She didn't really want to get into the subject, convinced she'd come across as some kind of native informant, but there was something about this case that needled her. There was this business about the adult victim: of the woman whose name and identity seemed to be of so little interest to anyone. Who would deny that the murder of these innocent girls at the hands of their own parents was utterly horrific? But wasn't the slaying of the woman who raised them equally horrific? Didn't it deserve some attention? What was this family's story behind the sensational headlines? How did the man secure immigration for an ex-wife *and* a second wife? She wasn't aware that ex-wives could be sponsored. And was he ever married to both of them, as Islamic custom still permitted—a practice that Ishaq-bhai had once joked about in a way she hadn't cared for, saying it was in decline "because our modern times were so expensive." Maybe the man managed to sponsor both women's immigration through some bureaucratic loophole? Some of the articles mentioned that he was wealthy and had come to Canada on an entrepreneurial visa.

Marisol's bushy ponytail slowly lifted from the fold-down table she'd been using as a headrest.

"Hello sleepyhead!"

"Hi." Marisol picked up her favourite Montreal Canadiens baseball cap and put it on, shielding her eyes from the sunlight streaming into the cabin.

"Are you alright?" Arubah asked.

"Coffee!" Marisol groaned.

"Another rough night?" Arubah eyed her over the reader.

"The only kind!" Marisol winked in a way Arubah didn't care to pursue.

Marisol stretched out her arms with a big yawn. She didn't have a stick of makeup on and her sweatshirt was pockmarked with coffee stains but none of this detracted from her beauty. Arubah caught guys drooling over her all the time. It wasn't PC of her, but she chalked up her friend's good looks to her mixed background, though Marisol laughed off the idea.

"Where are we?" Marisol rubbed traces of sleep from her eyes.

"I have no idea!" Arubah looked blankly at the cars and trucks along the highway running parallel to the tracks.

"OK, looks like we're maybe another forty minutes from Kingston, somewhere between Belleville and Napanee."

"How do you know that? Everything looks exactly the same!"

"Because I've made this journey a hundred million times!"

A soothing text alert, like a musical note, sounded off on Marisol's phone. She replied to the incoming text with a smile. "It's Mom! She's making jocon—it's a Guatemalan dish that's got a ton of cilantro, but she's nervous you won't like it because you know how Canadians can be really fussy about cilantro, saying it tastes like soap or something!"

"Are you kidding? It's practically the holy grail of Pakistani cuisine!"

Marisol resumed her texting.

"Forgot something?"

"Just to remind Mom about Elise—she's on a paleo diet."

Arubah bristled. Of course she is!

"And p s, Mom's got halal chicken for the jocon!" Marisol said.

Arubah breathed a sigh of relief. Things were admittedly easier when she didn't have to worry about making a nuisance of herself because of her own food restrictions.

"Please say thanks for me," she said.

"Done!" Marisol finished texting.

"Your parents seem so nice," Arubah sighed.

"Your mom's great, too. And her cooking is to die for!"

"Yeah, too bad none of it's rubbed off on me," Arubah said, holding out a packet of mixed nuts she had prepared for the trip.

"You've had a lot on your plate these last years."

"Mom sure has." Arubah checked her phone for missed calls.

"You too, Arubah. We could barely meet up for coffee because of all those hours you were putting in at Ginetti's. It's a good thing you've quit."

There was no doubt Arubah had worked her tail off. When she started uni, she had insisted on keeping her job to help out at home. *Economic self-sufficiency is the only path to a woman's freedom!* Raim Anwar had drilled this into her daughter's head from childhood. She herself could have taken handouts from her family in Pakistan, but she had fought hard to maintain her independence, even in the wake of finding herself a widow.

"Have you spoken to your mom lately?" Marisol asked.

Arubah calculated the time difference in Pakistan. Would she be awake or asleep at this hour, or was she taking the time to enjoy herself a little, reconnecting with old friends instead of sitting vigil at her father's side day and night?

"She seemed really happy about me going to Montreal with you."

"And how's your grandfather?"

"Not too great, by the sound of things."

"I'm sorry."

"I guess that's why Mom went back. It seems pretty serious."

Arubah studied the landscape outside, noting how the red leaves always fell first, leaving the land awash in yellows and browns. Her dad had clung to life just as stubbornly—at least till he made it to the hospital. But then he seemed to let go just as suddenly, like one of those leaves caught up in a tailwind. How had her mom managed to get through it all? It was one thing to be an immigrant and mourn the loss of a country, which she knew her mom did, even if she pretended not to; it was altogether another thing to become an immigrant-widow. Arubah wondered if her grandfather wasn't wrong to tell them to come back. Wouldn't life be easier for them both in Pakistan? She recalled how pampered they were on their summer visits; he even had a chauffeur to drive them around 24/7. It wasn't a long visit but she had felt more at home there than her mom did, which was odd because it was her first time in *the homeland*, as her grandfather called Pakistan in his old-fashioned way of speaking.

Marisol said something that Arubah didn't catch.

"We just passed a giant billboard for the Thousand Islands," Marisol repeated. "Remember those geography lessons in Junior High! The Thousand Islands-this, and the Canadian Shield-that! What a snore-fest!"

Arubah couldn't remember too much about her school life, even though it wasn't that long ago. She had sleep-walked through most of it, like her father's death had depleted her of oxygen. A senseless death, everyone had called it. A head-on collision on another stretch of the infernal Trans-Canada highway. To some it was the lifeline connecting the country's eastern and western extremes; to her it was a graveyard, a memorial site. Losing her dad had put her over a dangerous precipice. It was a wonder she had graduated high school at all. Then her mom pushed her to apply to university, for which she begrudgingly produced an overly emotional essay for the admissions process. She figured that would be the end of it, but the program coordinator was moved enough by her essay to overlook her spotty high school transcript.

"You know, if Professor Greenwood had been teaching those classes, I may have paid attention," Marisol prattled.

"Hmm?"

"I think he had mentioned something about the Thousand Islands—a creation story about the Great Spirit releasing a bundle into the river after being frustrated by warring tribes, and all of its contents formed the Islands, like a garden in the water." Marisol stopped to google something. "Here it is! The Matinouana, it's called. The Great Garden Spirit."

Arubah searched for signs of this water garden, but the train was sandwiched between two walls of chiselled rock, flashes of black and grey her only view. "I think my dad would have loved making this trip," she sighed. "He had a *Let's Discover Canada* phase . . . before he died. He was even saving up for one of those gigantic RVs!"

"I think our dads could have been besties. He has the travel bug, too. Mom, on the other hand," she sighed, "all she ever wants to do is go back to Guatemala to visit *familia*!"

"Have you been there?"

"Remember, I told you I had gone with my parents just after Junior High? They thought it was time for me to visit, but . . . I don't know how to explain it . . . it also made me sad."

"How come?"

"Because of what the country's been through, I guess. It's why mom's family came here. Things are way better now but when we visited it was like the country was still . . . I don't know how to put it: haunted, maybe?" Marisol turned towards the scenery rushing by.

They sank back into the rhythmic rocking of the train.

"You know what I remember most about Guatemala?" Marisol said, as the train moved through a dense copse of leggy pines. "The volcanoes and the butterflies! Everywhere you look, you see these volcanoes towering into the sky like giant green pyramids, and everywhere you go you have bright white butterflies for company. It's pretty magical!"

"Sounds like it! . . . And which part of the country is your mom from?" Arubah asked.

"Huehuetenango."

"Way-what?" Aruba struggled.

"Way-way-ten-ango. She was born not too far from a place called Aguacatan."

"Agua-ca-tan, like Pak-is-tan!"

"Muy bien, Señorita!"

"Graçias, Profesora Marisol!" Aruba smiled, thinking she would have taken Spanish as an elective if it weren't for the fact that she had set herself the goal of reading the Holy Quran in Arabic, compelled by the surah, "Those to whom we gave the Book, recite it as it should be recited."

"Anyway, it's called that because it's where the San Juan River begins," Marisol continued, "which is weird because it gushes right out of the foot of the mountain, like a pregnant woman whose water just broke. That's why the locals dubbed it Nacimiento—the birthplace. Anyway, Mom likes to say that her birthplace is *the birthplace!*"

The train slowed down, and Arubah was relieved when a bunch of people in their section prepared to disembark. They would have a quieter ride, and maybe even some space to talk about her ordeal. And Kashif.

"Kingston!" the automated voice recording announced.

"Hey, is anyone sitting here?" a Justin Bieber look-alike asked.

"No!" Arubah and Marisol moaned, hoisting their backpacks off the two extra seats some people had vacated at the last stop. Before they could commiserate, the Bieber look-alike signalled a friend, and the two freshmen made themselves right at home, launching into a bragging session about who was going to get more wasted on their pub crawl in Montreal.

"OMG!" Marisol mouthed, and drew out a novel titled *Palace of the Peacock*.

Arubah retreated to her notes. There was no way she was going to talk about such personal things with these two guys flanking them!

She opened up the course reader, when Marisol's text alert sounded off again. This time she detected it had a strange echo, like a water drop recorded in a cave or a well.

"Really!" Marisol scowled as she hit delete.

"Your mom?"

"No, just *this guy*! I don't know how the hell he got my number!"

Arubah was about to ask if it was the guy outside Professor March's class the other day but it was hard to talk over their new travel companions whose conversation was punctuated by intermittent shouts of "That's awesome!" and "No frickin' way!" So, she set the question aside for later and made another go of studying.

12

Marisol Martinez-Hamid paused at the top of the staircase in her family home. Like the river island's shifting sediment, the Montreal neighbourhood of Ville St-Laurent had morphed into the largest enclave of the Lebanese diaspora, the churches and rectories of the old parish standing defiantly amidst a multiethnic population. It wasn't one of the trendier districts, but when her father, Amin Hamid, was hired to teach applied sciences at the local college, the family transported themselves to a place dubbed *Ville Saint-Liban*. Though Amin didn't much care for these ethnic puns, he grew happily accustomed to the district's numerous perks, including the chance for his daughter to learn Arabic at a community centre, and the numerous specialty stores selling familiar delicacies from the Middle East.

Marisol heard her mother chatting with Arubah in front of a bookcase in the living room.

"So many books in so many languages, Mrs Martinez . . . and what's this one?" she heard Arubah ask.

"That's the *Popol Vuh*," Mrs Martinez explained. "The last part should sound like a soft breeze. Wuhhh."

"Wuhhh," Aruba gave it a try.

"Good! It's a sacred book of the Maya—the Quiche Maya. It's the Book of Origins."

"And these characters? Are they dragons?"

"That's the Q'uq'umatz, the Plumed Serpent, who helped create the earth with Huracan, the heart of the sky."

"That sounds familiar."

"It should! It's where the word *hurricane* comes from," Isabel explained patiently. "Those characters are part of the creation story. *The Book of Genesis*, the *Popol Vuh* . . . we all have our creation stories. And you'd be surprised how similar they are."

"Really?" Arubah pursued, as Marisol perched herself on a step, amused at her friend's endurance. "Well, the tree of life, for instance: this was the first thing the deities created to separate the sky from the earth; and then there's the great flood, the underworld, and even the concept of the soul or consciousness. The Mayan deities worked hard to create all this for human beings whom they first made out of wood and then, finally, corn."

She marvelled at her mom's ability to get round to the *Popol Vuh* with all their guests, like it was her mission in life to make people aware of it. And it was something of an inside joke that Isabel Martinez gave all the lectures in the family, so much so that she sometimes forgot which one of her parents was an actual professor.

"Corn is the most sacred food of the Maya! Even here, Indigenous peoples taught the settlers how to plant it. But what did people who showed so much hospitality get in return?" Marisol imagined Arubah biting down on a pen, like she did during exams. "Baroque theological cancer! That's what Miguel Angel Asturias—he's one of Guatemala's greatest authors—calls the Spanish conquest of America. And when I say America, I mean the whole continent: north, south, central and everything in between. Not the divided geography that the European cartographers have made of this continent, like a butchered turkey."

"OK, that's it!" Marisol resolved to rescue her friend when she heard the key turning in the front door. It was her father, a flurry of pine needles and soggy maple leaves blowing in behind him.

Amin Hamid held out some grocery bags as he disburdened himself of hat, coat, and shoes. "I forgot we had run out of pita, habibti. But I got a bit late because I bumped into Bassam—my old tax accountant. Remember him?" Amin hastily flung his coat over the finial. "He had the most upsetting news and we ended up talking for over an hour at the Café Beirut. Where's your mother? I have to tell her about it. You should all hear this."

"What happened? You look flushed," Isabel said.

"I'm all right, chérie, but I can't say the same for poor old Bassam. He and some other people were kicked out of the Tim Hortons—you know the one by the Indian supermarket, across from Metro Côte Vertu."

"Which people, Papa?" Marisol wondered if it was anyone she knew.

"Bassam was there by himself. There were a few other younger men sitting at another table. They turned out to be exchange students from Algeria, here for a semester at the University of Montreal. And there was another couple. The woman was wearing hijab, like Arubah."

"But Bassam isn't even a Muslim!"

"You know how it is! All the visibly Arab or Muslim customers were asked to leave."

"That can't be good for business in this town!" Marisol said and sat down by Arubah. "I mean, it's not called Ville St-Liban for nothing, is it!"

"And several of these people were elderly. Bassam swears all they were doing was having coffee and minding their own business!"

"I hope they told the manager where he could shove it!" Marisol hurled.

"I guess they did, in their own way." Amin rested his hands on the arms of the frayed recliner. "They asked why they were being singled out, and that they had as much right as any other paying customer to stay."

"And what did the manager do?" Arubah managed to get in.

"He insisted it was *his right* to refuse service to whomever he chose!" Amin's hands dropped to his lap.

"It may be his establishment but he could have a very serious lawsuit on his hands if it's a case of racial profiling!" Isabel said, drawing on her experience as a legal advocate for various causes, none of which were more important to her than the years spent seeking compensation for Mayan families displaced or killed over a major dam project. The massacres that had rocked the nation were the catalyst for the Martinez family to say *enough is enough* and make the migration north, but for Isabel the past was always present; she was one of those rare birds who felt migration was not so much a passport to move forward with immunity, as it was a contract to reach back with the privilege of distance.

"The police were called," Amin continued, "but they said it wasn't a criminal matter so there was nothing they could do."

"Fuckers!"

"Ay, Marisol!" Isabel admonished mildly. "Well, I hope Bassam isn't going to let this go! And I hope they took down the names of those police officers, too. They should be censured, you know."

"And did anyone else come to their defense?" Marisol asked. "Like any one of those *desirable* customers?"

"Bassam said they looked quite shocked, but no one said a word," Amin said. "The way the manager was behaving, they probably assumed he had some legitimate reason to feel threatened."

"OK, one person could be a potential criminal, or even a terrorist!" Marisol said, flushed. "But three sets of people! Câlisse!"

"I can tell you the worst part of it is how badly it's affected Bassam," Amin said, unwringing his hands and rubbing them against his jeans. "You should have seen the poor man. He was literally shaking when I bumped into him."

Marisol explained to Arubah that Bassam was from Syria, from a much older diaspora.

"Well, his family went to Brazil first, like your Uncle Masood," Amin qualified. "Then they made their way to Canada at the turn of the century . . . You know what he said to me before leaving?" Amin turned to his wife gravely: "El donya fanya."

Marisol whispered to Arubah: "Permanence is an illusion. An old Arabic saying."

"This is a clear case for the Quebec Human Rights Commission," Isabel said.

"It's true!" Arubah sat up. "Look what just happened *to me*—I mean, *at the mosque* around our neighbourhood. That should be a human rights issue, too." Arubah described the attack on Masjid Omar Bin Al-Hamad, which clearly hadn't made the Quebec news. "And now there are rumours flying around about Eid."

"Like what?" Marisol asked.

"Like maybe someone's planning a bigger attack. Eid's just around the corner, after all."

"When are these things going to be taken more seriously?" Isabel sighed.

"When someone gets killed! That's when!" Marisol said.

"Y'Allah!" Amin directed his gaze to the window but it had already gone dark. "Let's pray these are just rumours and nothing more." Marisol turned on a lamp when the doorbell rang, making them all jump.

"Quien es?" Isabel said.

Marisol sprang to her feet. "I almost forgot!"

"Elise?" Isabel said in a tone Marisol recognized as her mother's disapproval. Her mom still held Elise responsible for the year Marisol spent in Peru. She had gone there for a brief summer work-abroad program after high school but, as Isabel never tired of saying, *I didn't send my daughter all the way to Peru to end up in a romance with a Québécoise from Repentigny!* She had expected her dad to give her a harder time but, much like the way he had reacted to her coming out, he took it all in stride—though sometimes she got the impression he thought of Elise as a bug she just had to work out of her system.

"Bonjour tout le monde!" Elise called out in a singsong voice from the foyer. She handed a bottle of wine and a pie box to Marisol, and then proceeded to kiss everyone on the cheeks, eventually settling on Arubah.

"Aruba, like the Caribbean island!"

"No, it's Arubah, with an 'h'." Arubah was used to the confusion over her name, and with people's annoying tendency to sing that Beach Boys song. "*Not* like the island!"

"De toute façon!" Elise turned away, reaching into her tote bag and handing two small packets to Marisol and Isabel. "A gift from Uganda. Handmade by the women at the Shelter."

"C'est beau. Merci!" Isabel held up her earrings for everyone's appraisal before putting them on. Marisol did the same, explaining to Arubah that Elise's work as an NGO took her all over the world, and she had been living in Uganda for the past year.

"Amor, we should get dinner started," Isabel said to Amin who had retreated into a brooding silence since Elise's arrival.

"Ton papa: Ça va?" Elise asked as they left the room.

"He's just worried about a friend," Marisol said, switching back to English in the hope that Elise would follow suit.

Elise took the cue, turning to Arubah: "So, Marisol said you met at university?"

Arubah touched the gold earring under her hijab, a nervous twitch that had escalated ever since she was attacked. "Yes—in second year."

"And you're still in Women and Gender Studies, Marisol?" Elise asked.

"Yes, we both are," Marisol said.

"*Both* of you?"

"Yes, but," Arubah paused, thrown off by Elise's surprise, "lately I've been thinking about law."

"Well, this is new!" Marisol exclaimed.

"Yeah, I think I've just never really said it out loud before, but with everything that's going on these days . . . "

Marisol was about to ply Arubah with more questions when Isabel called her to the kitchen, giving Elise the time to wax nostalgic about Peru.

"Elise, why are you boring Arubah with all that?" Marisol said, returning with a plate of appetizers, which she placed on a colourfully embroidered ottoman.

"Don't mind me!" Arubah said, picking out a piece of stringy cheese from a platter.

Marisol hastened to wrap up Elise's story: "I had been wanting to do the Machu Picchu hike but a couple who said they'd go with me couldn't make it. Elise had been meaning to go but hadn't got round to it. And that's how we met. La fin! The End!"

"But tell her the rest!" Elise said impatiently. Before Marisol had a chance, she started up again: "The guide told us that when two strangers make the journey to the summit together, they wind up in each other's arms! And that's exactly what happened to us! We couldn't keep our hands off each other by the time we got back down the mountain!"

"Merde! Just drop it, OK!" Marisol snapped, precipitating a hushed exchange in French.

Arubah searched for something to preoccupy her, wishing she hadn't put the *Popol Vuh* back on the shelf. She wondered if Marisol and Elise would even notice if she got up to retrieve it, when Isabel reappeared from the kitchen, announcing that dinner was ready.

13

Frank checked his messages for the hundredth time. Nothing from Chris. And still no word from Cheryl about Thanksgiving. He hadn't planned on suggesting a family dinner, but there was no reason for all of them to suffer through Thanksgiving alone, was there? What was the harm in one family dinner, for old time's sake? And now that he had put it out there, he realized it was the best opportunity to share his good news with Chris. Maybe it could change things for them as a family, too. A fresh start, on all fronts.

He was about to cave in and call—give Cheryl a little push—when it occurred to him that it was pretty crappy of her not to tell him about her breakup with the Suit sooner. How long had she been hanging on to that particular bombshell? All he wanted when he got news of his remission was to share it with her, and yet she couldn't so much as tell him that the man she'd been shacking up with had moved out—moved out of *his* house, no less! Maybe this was why Chris was MIA. The Suit was no father-figure, that was for sure, but Chris was impressionable—nah, he was downright soft is what he was! And Cheryl was to blame for that! Always indulging. Never giving him any responsibilities.

It was a far cry from how he was raised. The Snyder men just got on with things. A good day was a day without a sound thrashing or a harsh word from Nick Snyder, his old man, who had never quite recovered from the time he lost everything to the "Great Flood." The flood had killed off the shoe factory where he'd worked most of his life, though some said the factories built on the riverbanks were at least partly to blame for the floods in the first place. Such insights were lost on the old man, who was about to make floor manager. It was a giant step for someone who had never been more than an underling in a town built on the industry of his ancestors, a long line of German tradespeople. Frank remembered his father bragging about how some products even bore a Made-in-Berlin label for a time and, like the town, he was determined to make a name for himself. He may very well have climbed that ladder and made good on the Snyder name, but how could anyone have known that Mother Nature herself would be conspiring against him!

"Yes, sirree, the Great Flood was the stuff of Snyder legend," Frank said aloud as the hope of a call from Cheryl dissipated with every passing second. He wondered if it would be far-fetched to say that the Great Flood had changed the direction of each of the Snyder men's lives, dragging his father down to a place of no-return, and lifting Frank up, towards a future that he couldn't have imagined without it. Even Chris, who rarely paid attention to *old people talk* had listened attentively to Frank's account of that legendary day, which could not have been more different than his father's embittered rants, typically washed down by a six-pack or a bottle of Canadian Club.

For Frank, the Great Flood saga was distilled through the eyes of a ten-year-old boy enamoured by the image of a lone police constable holding fast to his position while the river swallowed the streets. Frank had clipped the photo from a local newspaper and taped it onto his headboard the way other kids plastered their walls with rock-n-roll icons or hockey mascots. It was the image of that cop's devotion to the job that Frank held on to, while his father down-spiralled into a vortex of inebriated depression. And it was the image of that cop that helped him keep his head above water when the old man said Frank would amount to little more than the next generation of accursed Snyder men. In spite of his father's jabs, Frank was always careful not to bring up what had become the taboo subject of the Great Flood years.

The last time it had come up was also their last Thanksgiving together as a family, Frank realized. He remembered it well because their feisty great-aunt Louise had been there. And he vaguely recalled some tension between his sister Emmy and her daughter, Brittany, over this Joey-fellar. If he'd known that this would also be their last Thanksgiving, as a family, he'd have done a better job of burning it into his memory, and maybe even taking a picture or two. All he could remember now was how the Great Flood talk had got quashed before it started, thanks to good-old Aunt Louise.

———

"Enough of your damn snivelling, Nicky!" Aunt Louise snapped. "What's so damn special about a spring flood around here, anyway! Snyder stock have had to endure far, far worse!"

"Like what, Aunt Louise?" Brittany asked.

Aunt Louise nudged Chris for the salt. "Well, there was that dreadful war."

"Which one?" Brittany prodded gently.

"What does it matter which one!" Aunt Louise yelped. "No one should be treated like that! Like enemies in their own home!"

"She means the First World War," Emmy said as if she'd heard this story countless times.

"It sure must have been tough on the German families who'd settled here back then," Frank woke up to the conversation.

"Calling us collaborators and all sorts of rubbish!" Aunt Louise said, her fork banging against her plate. "Hadn't we done enough to prove our loyalty!"

Brittany playfully nudged her younger cousin but Frank was surprised by how intensely focused Chris was on his great-aunt.

"Who are *they* to change our name! We deserve that name! We built this town!"

"New Berlin!" Nick Snyder cried, startling everyone.

"Is that true, Mom?" Chris said.

"Don't ask me!" Cheryl replied. "I didn't grow up here!"

Frank explained that German immigrants had named the township New Berlin before the government changed it to Kitchener, hastening to add that Chris would have known this if he'd paid more attention in school.

"New Berlin's way cooler!" Chris ignored his dad. "What's up with that moronic *kitchen* name, anyway?"

"Don't be such a duffus!" Brittany scoffed.

"Anyway, Aunt Louise's generation would have liked the name to have some connection to the old country," Frank said. "And Kitchener was an old British war hero, for your information."

"Who are *they* to tell us this isn't *our* land!"

"What's Aunt Louise on about now?" Chris looked to his cousin for an explanation, despite their continual sparring.

"She gets things mixed up," Brittany groaned. "She thinks *all* the old families who came here are the same, but some came directly from Germany and others came from places like Pennsylvania—at least the Mennonites were already in the US before they came here. Right, Uncle Frank?"

"I believe so."

"And *they* were the ones who bought most of the land around the Grand River." Brittany speared a roasted carrot. "Land that wasn't theirs to buy! Thousands—no, hundreds of thousands of acres—that was treaty land!"

"Not this again!" Emmy said, replenishing her father's gravy.

"Well, it's true, Mom!" Brittany pushed away her plate. "Joey said it belongs to the Six Nations—to the Haudenosaunee!"

Chris shrugged off the bowl of green beans Cheryl was attempting to pass him.

"Yes, and aren't we lucky to live by all these farms!" Cheryl chimed, giving up on the vegetables making it to her son's plate. "There'd be no Thanksgiving dinner without them! No potatoes. No corn. And no green beans."

"Gross!" Chris hurled.

"The Mennonites weren't the first farmers around here, Aunt Cheryl!" Brittany fired rapidly, warding off another interruption.

Emmy reached for the bottle of wine and poured herself and Cheryl another glass.

"Anyway," Brittany caught her breath, "my point is that it's the Mennonites who are up to their eyeballs in land-treaty disputes because they bought this land from white speculators who had no business selling it in the first place!"

"What's your interest in all this stuff, Brittany?" Frank had never given much thought to the land claim issues surrounding the GR, even after he had been called in as part of the OPP presence during what had become a major standoff over one of those disputes. It had all happened an hour south of Kitchener, which seemed far enough removed from *their* stretch of the GR to be someone else's issue— someone else's war.

"Because of her old boyfriend, Joey, that's who!" Emmy answered on her daughter's behalf. "Joey bear-clan."

"He's part of the Bear *Clan*, Mom! That's not his name!"

"Bear-claw!" Chris mocked, brandishing a fork.

"Watch me turn this gravy boat on your head!"

Emmy pressed her forehead. "For heaven's sake, you two! Let your Grandpa and Aunt Louise eat in peace!"

"Do you know what else Joey told me?" Brittany took back the reigns defiantly. "*Everything* here's stolen. Even names!"

"That's stupid!" Chris said.

"Even the Grand River!" Brittany persevered.

"That river's cursed, I tell you!" Nick Snyder muttered through a set of loose dentures.

Frank wasn't sure what this little tiff between Emmy and her daughter was about, but anything concerning the river was of interest to him. "Go on, then, Brittany."

"Nothing, Uncle Frank!" Brittany projected a death-stare at her mom. "Joey said the Grand River's had a bunch of different names, and he personally wishes it could be called Bear River."

"You don't say!" Frank said, suddenly feeling the urge to get back out on the river.

"Joey says without the bear there's no one to protect the river."

"So how about those Raptors, eh!" Emmy held up her glass. "Does anyone think they'll win another championship?"

"Oh! And there's another name, too!" Brittany ignored her mother. "It's too hard to pronounce, so I won't even try. But I think he said it had something to do with those trees . . . "

"The scrawny looking pine trees the artists like to paint?" Cheryl said a little tipsily.

"No, the really big ones that grow along the river," Brittany said.

"Willows?" Frank said.

"That's right! I think it means *the place where willows grow*."

"You know, that makes total sense." Frank chewed over this latest revelation. He felt it was the first name that truly captured the river's character. He loved to doze off under the shade of those weeping willows, or stare at their distinctive scarlet roots, which glistened like red licorice strings, the kind he and Emmy fought over when they were kids, under the riverbed shallows.

"Maybe that should have been the city's name! Willowtown. Or Willowdale," Cheryl said.

"How about Willowsburg?" Frank got in on the name game.

"It *is* nicer than Kitchener," Emmy conceded.

Brittany fiddled with a beaded earring dangling off her left ear. "I think we're missing the point here."

"Hey, Dad said you should never *dis* a war-vet!" Chris fisted his cousin.

"Jeez, Chris," Brittany rubbed her arm, "do you even know which wars your dad was talking about!"

"Jeez, Brittany! Do you even know where you got those ugly earrings!"

"That's enough, Chris!" Frank intervened. "And you're not entirely wrong, son. Kitchener was an officer of the highest order for the British Imperial army. He was a veteran—a highly decorated one—*of his day*."

"Actually, Uncle Frank, Joey said Kitchener was a war criminal doing the Empire's dirty work all over Africa."

"Sounds like someone's missing her ex!" Cheryl trilled.

"It's Joey-this. And Joey-that!" Emmy grumbled. "See what I have to put with!"

———

It had been a doozy of a family dinner, that much Frank remembered. Everyone was uncharacteristically chatty, so much so that Thanksgiving had barely come up save for a half-hearted round of the *who-gives-thanks-for-what-game* initiated by Emmy. His old man had not disappointed, sheepishly holding up a glass of gin he had swindled from Emmy's liquor cabinet. And Emmy, ever the conciliator, chose to ignore him and say something redeeming about family ties. Brittany, he was quite certain, had lobbed another grenade at their German ancestors or said something that sent Emmy reaching for a Tylenol. All this he recalled quite clearly, but for the life of him he couldn't remember what Chris or Cheryl had said they were thankful for. Worse than this, he didn't recall what *he* had said. He wasn't much for speeches and the old man hadn't raised him to be sentimental but it seemed like a missed opportunity now. Granted, he had no idea what was in store for them back then—the cancer, the divorce, the end of the world as he knew it. But did he really need to be at death's door to tell the people in his life what they meant to him?

Frank looked at the clock, resigned to Cheryl not calling. Resigned to spending another holiday alone. Was this payback for all those years Cheryl had accused him of putting her last, of effectively "cheating on her" with his job, as she liked to say?

But this wasn't any other holiday on any other year, was it? It was the year he had been given a new lease on life, and wasn't that worth something? Wasn't that worth some expressions of gratitude and thanks?

14

Kashif owed Nasser one. If he hadn't made insinuations about *that cop*, Kashif wouldn't have had the nerve to call Frank. He wasn't expecting him to suggest meeting so soon—on Thanksgiving, no less. Most people wouldn't think of a casual conversation with an off-duty cop a stroke of good luck, but Kashif didn't think he merited the universe's attention much less divine intervention.

Even his interest in the police academy had presented itself haphazardly, from an evening chat show. The guests were discussing police recruitment in the Greater Toronto Area. Two high schoolers described the heavy police presence outside their schools, and it made him think of the number of times he'd been trailed by patrol cars on his way to the gas station. He'd never been arrested or anything, but what one of the experts said really hit home: "What kind of person do you want to be? The kind that helps keep your streets safe because they're your streets, or the kind who thinks they'll never be safe because they're your streets?"

"So, that's pretty much how the application process works. And once your medical is cleared, you'll be able to take the other tests," Frank said between tentative sips of a chai latte. "Anyway, I don't see why your medical should be a problem." Frank set down the tea with a grimace.

"Has the milk soured? I hate it when that happens!" Kashif said, surprised by Frank's choice, imagining cops only drank coffee—plain, strong and bitter.

"No, it's not that." Frank paused. "I just remembered this old guy at the mosque. He didn't like his tea being compared to *this stuff*! He had a point!"

"Um, which mosque? The one that got attacked?" Kashif sat up, on high alert.

"Right! I was meaning to tell you about it," Frank said good-naturedly. "It was the strangest thing, but I just happened to be driving out that way the day we'd met at the hospital, so I figured what's the harm in stopping to check things out."

"Did you talk to anyone there?" Kashif asked as casually as he could.

"Yup! And I may have mentioned you in passing, by the way. They seemed to know you—at least the younger guy in the suit did."

Nasser! Kashif's throat constricted.

Frank leaned back in his chair and pressed his hands against the table, a gesture Kashif imagined him making in an interrogation office, though he didn't even know if Frank was *that* kind of cop. "You were right about the place taking a real beating. Though much of the mess had been cleaned up by civically-minded volunteers, like your good self, by the time I got there. I was just mildly curious about it, really— since I was passing by and all."

"And did anyone ask why you were there? Like that guy in the suit?"

"Just briefly, but since the police had already come and gone, no one really paid me too much mind."

"So, you didn't have a chance to talk to the police, either? About any leads? Anything like that?" Kashif pushed.

"Nah! Like I said, they'd already gone; and they have a pretty standard procedure for vandalism cases, and even these investigations take quite a bit of time. If there's something to report, I am sure your Director-fellow will hear of it soon enough. For my part, there's really not much else to report!"

Kashif wanted to get Frank's take on the letter and the earlier threats against the mosque but recalled what Nasser had said about none of this having been made public. Besides, Nasser seemed to have a pretty low opinion of the police, so at least for now there was no point dragging Frank into their business any further. At least it was good to know there'd be *some* kind of inquiry.

Kashif found Frank distracted by a group of guys sitting in the far corner of the coffee shop. They were mainly Sikh, as well as a few other brown kids who weren't wearing turbans. They were pretty animated but seemed harmless enough.

"Um, will you be going back to work soon?" he ventured.

"We'll see . . . Though we're getting a bit off track, aren't we! We're here to talk about *your* police career, not mine!"

Kashif liked the sound of that. A career. His dad had his taxi job. His mom had her factory job. He had his job at the gas station. But a *career*? And the way Frank said it—like it was a done deal.

"Um," he started but was interrupted by a ring.

Frank studied his call display. "Excuse me, I have to take this!"

Kashif nodded, thinking of the time he'd teased his dad for choosing the same retro ring for his smartphone.

"Brittany?" Frank said. "This is a surprise!"

Kashif browsed his social media feed in the effort not to eavesdrop.

"Chris? What about him?" Frank set aside the tea. "You mean he showed up unannounced . . . in Kitchener? . . . for Thanksgiving? . . . Why? . . . Girlfriend? What girlfriend!"

Kashif snuck a peak. Something was up.

"I'm sorry, he's at *whose* place? . . . You're engaged! . . . Your mom never mentioned—oh, *that Joey!*"

Even from across the table Kashif could hear the woman's voice go up an octave.

"I'm confused: why did Chris end up crashing with you guys? You know how hard I've been trying to get a hold of that boy!"

Kashif wondered if all fathers around the planet referred to their sons as "that boy" when they were in their bad books. His dad was no exception, only he said it in Urdu when he was especially pissed. Any time Kashif heard the words, "wo larka," he knew it was time to make himself scarce.

"Sorry? . . . A fight with his girlfriend? . . . Well, that doesn't seem like a reason to be hassling you . . . Listen, just put him on the phone, would ya . . . Where is he, then?"

Kashif stole another look but Frank was too preoccupied to notice.

"Jeez Louise! . . . Chris *said what!*" Frank rested his elbow on the table. "I didn't raise him to be such a . . . Well, tell Joey it was real stand-up of him to get that scoundrel to the bus station in spite of . . . Yeah, sure, I can tell your mom you've got a good one there! . . . And thanks for letting me know, eh! . . . Yup, you take care, too, Brittany."

Kashif reconciled himself to cutting their meeting short when Frank set his phone on the table, scrolled through his contacts and clicked on the name Chris. A photo of a guy, about Kashif's own age, appeared in the profile picture while a number dialled. It was upside down but Kashif could make out the family resemblance, though Chris's hair was darker than Frank's and his jawline not as angular—more Chris Hemsworth, less Clint Eastwood. Unlike Hemsworth in what Kashif considered to be his greatest role as Thor, Frank's son sported one of those faded hair styles Kashif detested—all shorn off on the sides but longer on top.

"Leave me alone or leave me a message," a voice with none of Thor's bass tones came on speaker mode. Frank examined the image like evidence in a cold case. "My son."

"Is your son a cop, too?" Kashif rambled. "I mean, if my dad were . . . "

"It doesn't always work out that way." Frank redialled but shut off the recorded greeting in midsentence. "And what about you, kid? What does your old man do?"

"He's a taxi driver. I'm really not sure what he's doing now, though." Kashif traced his fingers along the grooves of some misshapen letters scratched into the table. "I haven't seen him in a while."

"Oh?"

"He and my mom are . . . I guess they're separated."

"While she's been dealing with the cancer?"

"Yup."

"That's rough," Frank crossed his arms. "Believe me, I know."

"I think he's with someone else—another woman!" Kashif turned red, ashamed. He considered what his father had done a *gunha*—a sin, the shame of which he and his mother had to bear. He had never told anyone about it. Not even Zafar.

"Look, son," Frank set his hands on the table. "I can appreciate your thinking the worst of your dad right now, especially when your mom's so sick and all. But if you want to be a cop, a good cop, then you've got to be ready to hear all sides of the story. Your dad's side."

Frank's point seemed reasonable enough. But his dad wasn't some random suspect in police custody. How could he keep his emotions out of it?

"I mean, look at my kid. He's been MIA for weeks and he's owed a swift kick in the ass, but I'd still give my right arm to talk to him! Even though he's been lying about things, lately." Frank paused to look at the guys at the other table. One of them had sprung to his feet, talking and gesticulating at great speed. "What the devil!"

"Sorry? You were saying?" Kashif pushed, figuring if the coffee shop weren't so deserted Frank wouldn't have paid much attention to those guys who, upon second glance, looked more like a group of teens.

"Uh, right," Frank resumed. "I was saying my son's been acting a bit odd lately. Like bringing up all this ancient history about some stand-off with native groups. Unless Joey, my niece's boyfriend, brought it up. I mean, Brittany mentioned he's from one of the Reserves out there."

Kashif wasn't sure what Frank meant by *out there*. Aside from a few school trips outside the city limits and a rare family trip to Niagara Falls, he'd never been more than a few hours west or east of Toronto.

"Do you know that was one of the longest standoffs in Ontario?" Frank kept his focus on the group of teens. "Anyway, it was over land marked for another one of those cookie-cutter housing developments along the Grand River. The native groups set up a blockade at the entrance to the construction site, saying it was all still theirs by treaty. So, what's new, eh?"

Kashif sat up, anticipating a good police story.

"I don't think the OPP's ever amassed in such numbers, before or since, I can tell you that firsthand! What's it to Chris, though? He's never cared about that stuff!" Frank closed the lid on the tea. "Look, I don't know about all this treaty business, but I thought I raised my kid to know better! At least to know better than to disrespect someone in their own house!"

"Uh, what about the standoff?" Kashif wished they could get back to the policing stuff. Did they have to do things like form a human shield? Did they break up any fights?

"Well, things got really stirred up when the local residents held their own rally because some members of the Six Nations also saw fit to set up blockades along some major roadways. And don't ask me who makes up the Six Nations, but I figure one must be Mohawk, because that's Joey's background, apparently." Frank paused and rubbed his chin.

"Was your son involved in the protest?"

Frank laughed. "Hell, no! He was practically still in diapers, like you! That's why I just can't make sense of this. Since when has my kid cared about politics! It seems more like he was *looking* to pick a fight with Joey, who, as my niece just informed me, is as good as family now."

"Did things get resolved? In terms of the standoff, I mean?"

"Good question! There were lawsuits on one side, boycotts on the other, court injunctions, arrests—even a State of Emergency. I think the government ended up paying the local business owners pretty generous compensation for lost revenue. It's the least they're owed, considering they're just decent, hard-working folks who took a real hit on account of the blockade, you know. But beyond that, I don't know if anything's been what you might call *settled* yet. That kinda depends on which side you talk to, I guess. Ours or theirs."

Kashif wondered which one of those sides *he* belonged to, at least in Frank's eyes.

"Truth be told, most of us just want the same damn thing: we want to canoe down our rivers and walk along our creeks without having to buy a goddamn golf membership or McMansion to do it! . . . Or maybe that's all *I* want, anyway!" Frank brought up Chris's picture and touched the screen with his finger before shoving the phone back into his pocket. "Brittany said Chris has bussed it back to Toronto, so he'll be home soon enough. Though I'm not sure I'll be calling again. There's only so many times—" Frank changed direction: "Well, let's just say it's time for Chris to reach out to the MWGHL now."

"The what?"

"It's an inside joke. I call myself the Man-Who-Gave-Him-Life!"

"It sounds like Mughal!" Kashif spelled it out: "M-U-G-H-A-L! The Muslims who built the Taj Mahal! My dad says we should be proud to come from a long line of Mughals, because they were the last empire to resist the British! I guess you could say that was another kind of standoff, right!"

Kashif was pleased with his analogy, wishing his dad was around to hear it, especially because it seemed lost on Frank, who was already standing up and putting on his jacket, his gaze still fixed on the teens.

"It sounds like they're on the verge of a shootout the way they're carrying on!" Frank said sternly.

Kashif felt the need to come to the kids' rescue. They had been speaking in Hindi, and he got the gist of their heated debate about video games. "Uh, Frank, I don't think they speak English," he fibbed, because he'd never met a desi kid from the burbs who didn't speak English. "I can talk to them, though." He took charge and walked over to the group before Frank could reply.

The boys were quick to apologize for being rowdy, but Kashif assured them it wasn't a big deal. "Though ranking *Call of Duty* above *Grand Theft Auto*—now *that's* a criminal offense!" he joked, setting off a round of laughter and good-humoured banter.

Kashif left them to debate the merits of graphic updates and multi-player functionality and looked for Frank. He was already waiting by the door, his legs set apart in an inverted V, arms slung down, hands perpendicular to hips, and just for a moment Kashif was transported to an open savannah, covered in a veil of dust and grit, facing off the enemy. Ready for a fast draw.

15

A rubah and Elise took their seats at the table, every inch of which was covered with dishes handpainted in arabesque motifs. "Is that Lebanese or Guatemalan?" Arubah's mouth watered as she studied one of the more unusual platters of rice.

"That's native wild rice—manoomin," Isabel explained. "Some Anishinaabe say that it's the manoomin that brought them here, to the land where food grows on water. I always serve it at Thanksgiving."

"Alors, bon appetît, tout le monde!" Amin exclaimed, setting down the last of the dishes.

"Happy Thanksgiving!" Elise toasted salubriously.

"This is an anti-Thanksgiving house, Elise!" Marisol said, parodying her mother. "Mom says 'Thanksgiving is a colonial celebration of cultural genocide'!"

"OK, Marisol, let everyone enjoy their meal!"

"Indeed!" Amin cut in. "Here, we always give thanks. For our many blessings. For this incredible meal. For this smart-aleck daughter and, most importantly, for the opportunity to spend time with cherished family and friends."

"And let's give thanks for this truly eclectic group," Isabel held up her glass. "It's like the United Nations tonight."

"Like the true face of Canada!" Amin said.

"Comme un vrai Québec!" Elise regaled.

"Like, you guys are corny as hell!" Marisol tapped the rim of her mother's glass with her own, setting off a timpani of clinking glasses.

Everyone took a focused sip of their drinks, hesitant to be the first to dig in. Elise broke the mannered impasse. "I was telling Arubah how Marisol and I met but I don't think I know how you and Isabel met," she said as Amin stacked a few rice-stuffed bundles of dolmas on her plate.

"Well, as I'm sure you know, Isabel's family came to Canada as refugees from Guatemala," Amin explained. "And I came on my own, from Lebanon, after the war. We met at the university when I was finishing a second doctorate."

Arubah almost choked on a chicken bone. Two doctorates! It was hard enough to get through an undergrad degree!

"Amin should have got an academic position right away. He was fully qualified, but you know how this system can be," Isabel sighed. "Then Marisol came along, shall we say a bit unexpectedly, and he wound up keeping his teaching position at the college. Kids have a way of making choices for you."

"Right! It's all my fault!" Marisol gave a dramatic eye-roll.

Amin explained that Isabel had to leave for Guatemala shortly after they met because the reparations case she was working on had reached a critical juncture. Somehow, they managed to keep in touch, almost daily, while she was away. "And the rest, as they say, is history!" he finished up, taking his wife's hand in his.

"Á l'amour!" Elise waved her glass at Marisol.

They all raised their glasses for a second toast, the turn in conversation eventually landing on the subject of university studies.

"Marisol said you've been working on a paper about Quebec?" Isabel inquired, serving Arubah another generous spoonful of jocon.

"Actually, it's more like I'm trying to pin down my final paper topic for our Gender and Social Justice course."

"It's a great topic," Marisol interjected. "We even had a bit of a showdown with the prof!"

"My daughter arguing with the professor? I can't imagine!" Amin needled.

"So, what is the Quebec connection?" Isabel asked.

"Professor March used the example of that horrible case," Marisol answered. "You know the one involving the whole family?"

"Que c'était barbarique!" Elise exclaimed.

"I'm sorry, it's not a very happy dinner topic," Arubah said.

"No, I'd like to hear your take on it, Arubah. And about this show-down with the professor," Amin said.

"Well, Marisol's the one who had the courage to ask Professor March the tough questions. But it was another aspect of the case that I found interesting. Like why the focus was on the daughters but not the older woman who also got killed that night. And why the daughters were referred to as Canadians but not the rest of the family."

"Right!" Marisol said. "That's kind of what bothered me about the lecture, too. So many things were glossed over just to make the point about it being an honour killing!"

"Well, you know we have to condense a lot of material for those lectures," Amin came to the professor's defense. "It's not easy to cover a topic from every possible angle."

"I remember that case!" Elise set down her fork. "Didn't it all start with one of the daughters wanting to run away with her boyfriend?"

"Let's say all of that was true. But haven't we heard this story before? Just recently a man killed his girlfriend and her daughters. It was a triple murder, similar to this one. That wasn't called an *honour killing* or a *barbaric cultural practice*."

"A father killing his daughters because they're just dating? That's hardly common!" Elise argued.

"Well, we don't know that because cases involving white dudes aren't pursued in the same way. We're simply told the perpetrator is a nut-job or a repeat offender! The case is deemed sensational, tragic, whatever, and we move on."

"I was just reading that one woman in Canada is killed every six days," Isabel said gravely. "And it's usually by a man who knows her. A husband, an ex, a boyfriend—"

"And *they* aren't called honour killings!" Marisol continued breathlessly. "Mama, what's the term for claiming you were led to commit a crime?"

"Defence of provocation."

"That's right! I was reading that, back in the day, defense of provocation was part of English civil law, justifying things like a man's right to take the life of an adulterous wife, or at least have a murder sentence reduced to manslaughter if he could prove he was justifiably provoked. Anyway, doesn't that sound a bit like an honour killing to you?"

"Didn't I always say you should apply to law school!" Isabel commented.

"I'm still figuring things out, Mama. But you'll be pleased to know that there will be at least *one* lawyer at this table." Marisol tilted her fork at Arubah.

Arubah blushed. "Um, I don't know about that. I like Women and Gender Studies as a major, but I've been seeing it more as a foundation to something—maybe law. I don't know," she paused. "It's just a thought right now."

"It's a good thought," Isabel crooned.

"And what do you think about this case?" Elise capitalized on the shift of focus to Arubah. "Do you agree that there are no honour killings in Muslim societies?"

"I never said that, Elise!" Marisol said indignantly. "I said that honour killings are not exclusive to *one* culture! And, more often than not, they're rooted in old tribal customs and mentalities. That's all!"

"Isn't that the same thing?"

"I don't know. Do we condemn Christianity because hazing in frat houses happens in predominantly Christian societies?"

"I would be interested in Arubah's perspective, too." Isabel mediated. "Since you're both taking the class, I mean."

"Well, I don't really know anything about Islamic law," Arubah said, feeling like she was the one on the witness stand now. "But the case seems extremely sensational and there is a lot we don't know. To start, it involved more than one perpetrator. In fact, I've been reading some of the reports released after the trial, and it seems that the woman, his second wife, had a lot to do with it. At the very least, she was his accomplice and must be deeply disturbed. I mean, she would have to be to have killed her own children!"

"That's exactly my point!" Marisol piggy-backed off Arubah's argument. "The case is so complicated because there are way too many unanswered questions. Like Arubah said, this other woman has been treated as an accessory, but no one seems to be calling *her* motives into question."

"Wasn't the first wife living with them?" Isabel asked.

"Under the very same roof!" Marisol answered.

"I think I heard some talk about this man," Amin said. "Nothing substantiated. More like local gossip that he may have been involved in weapons manufacture and maybe even in arms-dealing. For which side, I'm not sure, but he definitely had the means, and maybe the insider connections, to expedite his immigration and get himself out of his country when he had to." Amin looked up to four sets of eyes on him. "Well, who knows? These are just rumours."

"OK, but what about these poor girls?" Elise asked. "Whatever all the other circumstances may be, the father confessed! He described his disgust over his daughters' behaviour. *He* even called it an honour killing, from what I remember!"

Marisol jumped at this: "No one is saying the man shouldn't be locked up for life! But are you telling me that daughters and wives aren't killed by men around here for all kinds of reasons: the wrong look, the wrong tone, the wrong boyfriend, a bad day, a good day! Not just killed but abused and molested and all kinds of gruesome things! We're not arguing for their deportation. We're not accusing them of tainting our great democracy. We aren't holding a microscope to their beliefs. Most of them get a slap on the wrist. And they may be branded as social deviants but they're not seen as *culturally* defective!"

Isabel cut in: "It is true that we enter very dangerous territory when we accuse people for a set of behaviours for which we aren't prepared to scrutinize ourselves."

"I guess it all depends," Amin said, more to himself than the others at the table, "on who we define as *we*. On who we define as *ourselves*. It's something we're all struggling with these days . . . "

"But that's my point, Papa! If it weren't for this kind of blanket assumption about Muslims, would it be acceptable for some Tim Hortons manager to feel it's OK to throw out a group of customers—!"

"Ah, look! It's snowing!" Amin exclaimed, as if he didn't want to rehash things.

"Already?" Isabel got up and stood by the window. Arubah, Elise and Marisol followed, everyone looking a little relieved to escape the political turn the discussion had taken.

Arubah watched the family gather around the window, Amin's arm around Marisol's shoulder. She wondered if her own father would have been the type to share a glass of wine with her, or if he would have raised her more strictly. She had assumed he would be the latter but realized she had no basis for arriving at such a conclusion. The only male role models she now had were the imams and other men at the mosque—men who might go so far as to spurn the likes of Amin Hamid for his "overly liberal" ways. Even *she* couldn't believe he was so open to Marisol's relationship with Elise—to Marisol's *other side*.

Arubah offered to help clear up when Marisol said she'd walk Elise to the subway, but the hosts insisted they had everything under control. She thought she could have a closer look at that book, the *Popol Vuh* again, when another spine ensconced among a row of Arabic titles caught her eye.

"Ana Hiya Anti," she sounded out the words in the title, pleased with her pronunciation since she had started taking Quranic classes at the Centre.

Arubah examined the book cover. A woman's silhouette inside a doorway was superimposed upon a sepia-toned photograph of an abandoned building standing partly in shadow and partly in light.

Still mouthing the words, Ana Hiya Anti, she opened the book to the first page, which noted the English translation: *I Am You.*

I Am You, Arubah read the title again, tracing her finger along the figure of the silhouetted woman.

16

Kauthar was loathe to stay in the cramped lobby for longer than was needed to check the mailbox. Run-ins with other residents were always a potential hazard, but a dizzy spell forced her to linger. She sat down on a bench and eyed the elevators, relieved to see them taking longer to come down.

It had been a while since she had hung around the lobby for any length of time. She could count at least two large stains on the ceiling. The carpet was faring little better in spite of the plastic runners laid to catch the soggy grime of foot traffic. And the one decorative feature, an artificial ficus tree, was covered in a white, sticky film. Kauthar reckoned the ficus had been a tenant in the building almost as long as she, unable to remember a time when it wasn't standing in the corner, always neglected and alone.

Kauthar tensed up at the sight of one of the elevators heading down to the ground floor, where it ejected an adolescent girl. Her grip tightened over a bundle of flyers as the girl stopped to smooth down her already iron-straight hair, making Kauthar think of a doll she used to play with. It had a sheet of shiny blond hair, just like this girl. The doll's hair was about the only thing that remained intact, all of the other doll-parts either broken or misshapen.

Kauthar exhaled as the girl exited the building, her light, youthful steps blaring at her like an enemy's bugle declaring she had lost the battle against Time. Isn't that what Dr Eleniak had implied at their last appointment?

"Your body has failed to respond favourably to the last round of treatment," he'd announced.

At the time, Kauthar wasn't sure if she had understood correctly. *Failed* seemed to suggest it was *her* fault the treatment had not worked. Had she done something wrong? The question made her regret leaving Kashif in the waiting room that morning. Still, she was determined to take charge: "And eating? The tube?"

"Patience and persistence, Ms Siddiqui."

"How long?" Kauthar asked again, wishing the doctor's answers could be delivered to her in black and white, not with these insufferably colourful expressions.

"Let's just say it will be a while before you're out of the woods."

It had been a few weeks since her last appointment and the shocking news that they would not be taking out the feeding tube for the foreseeable future, and that she might never recover the ability to eat or swallow. She would likely never be *normal* again.

She hadn't told anyone the devastating news, though whom did she have to tell but Kashif? And how could a mother give a son such news? Then there was the other matter of her suspicions that Kashif was in communication with his father again. It was not that she was against the idea of father and son reconnecting. That was the natural order of things. It was just that she couldn't bear the news of her illness reaching Hassan. It was bad enough being dependent on him to keep the household running. If she had told him about the cancer, he might even have left that woman—*that gori*—and come back home out of a sense of duty and obligation . . . Was she being foolish? Maybe she *should* have told him about it right from the start! But how could she wake up every morning to a man looking at her with pity or, worse, disgust—a wife disfigured, inside and out, by disease.

Kauthar jumped at the sensation of something warm on her shoulder. It was Tasneem and one of her daughters. Of all the neighbours she wished to avoid! The last thing she could handle was feeling scandalized or judged. Why had Hassan put her in this shameful predicament! And why wasn't Kashif here? He hardly spent any time at home anymore.

"Kashif kidhar hai?" Kauthar asked after Kashif's whereabouts, overcome by another dizzy spell.

Mother and daughter exchanged concerned looks.

"It's Thanksgiving, Kauthar-Aunty—he can't be too far. Not much is open today." Kauthar saw a pair of soft brown eyes staring down at her. She couldn't be sure which one of the twins it was: Bina or Banu.

"Listen, Kauthar-bhain, you don't want to catch a cold. Too much draft." Tasneem helped Kauthar to her feet and back to the elevators. "Why are you down here so late, anyway?"

Kauthar had come to check the mailbox, forgetting it was the long weekend. She'd been forgetting a lot of things lately.

She accepted Tasneem's support and they rode up the elevators together, but something was amiss when they got out on what she assumed was her floor. For one, the light across from the elevator was brighter than the one on her floor, and there was an intense smell of incense emanating from one of the apartments. She had stopped lighting incense when Management had circulated a notice prohibiting the use of such "inflammables" after one of the apartments had caught fire because of a burning candle.

"Come, Aunty-ji," Kauthar heard Tasneem's daughter say in a gentle way that reminded her of her former co-worker Arubah. She missed that young woman's incessant chatter about the university. She wondered whether she had managed to complete her studies.

Tasneem fiddled with the lock and guided Kauthar inside, the heady scents of rose and sandalwood a dead giveaway that this was not her apartment. Kauthar was about to say as much when a naked figure wrapped in a towel darted out of a room and across the hall.

"Qassam-se, Bina!" Tasneem shouted.

"I'm not psychic, Ammi!" a woman's voice yelled from one of the rooms. "You didn't tell me someone's coming!"

"I apologize for my daughter, Kauthar-bhain," Tasneem said

breathlessly as she manoeuvred Kauthar onto a worn, grey sofa with one hand while straightening out her shalwar kameez.

Kauthar blinked like a startled butterfly, distracted by her new surroundings.

"May Allah grant us patience with that one! Sometimes I wonder why she observes purdah at all! I'm telling you that last trip to the Gulf is what did it! The way the women move about in their long black robes like floating princesses! But I was dead-set against it, you know." Tasneem talked a mile a minute, as was her habit. She picked up a Kashmiri shawl draped on the sofa, the gold thread and elaborate hand-embroidered designs such a contrast to the shabby furniture. "Qassam-se, I still don't fully understand it! If they wanted to wear chador, like some of our own women back home, I could understand, but—"

"Your daughters are very beautiful, mash'allah," Kauthar interrupted Tasneem's chatter.

The compliment provided the briefest lull before Tasneem started up again: "She's a sly one, that girl, always going for maximum shock value! Now, our Banu: she's the thoughtful one! Always studying, always thinking things through careful-careful," Tasneem beamed. "She's going to be a doctor, you know!"

Kauthar nodded no—she didn't know. And she wondered why Tasneem was behaving like they were old friends when her neighbour had never taken more than what felt like a charitable interest in her. Now here she was, in Tasneem's home, on Tasneem's sofa, listening to Tasneem's private family affairs.

Tasneem lifted up the dupatta draped lightly over her head and placed it around her neck. "Zia, their father, should have tried harder to talk them out of it, if you ask me! In Saudi they'd blend in, but here? We don't want our daughters to be kicked off buses or banned from government buildings because of a niqab. Don't we have enough obstacles to contend with in this land!"

Tasneem threw up her hands in a V-shape that reminded Kauthar of the birds taking flight from her balcony. "But after a lengthy consultation with the maulana, Zia gave them his blessing. After all, the temptations here are as great as the obstacles, he said! If they need something to help keep them pure, then so be it . . . Though, if you ask me, that maulana is a new Wahabi recruit whom I don't much care for."

"Ammi, phone!" A young woman sauntered into the room wearing a long blue kaftan with white brocade, her long waves of black hair still wet from the shower. "It's Nasim."

"Nasim calling so late?" Tasneem snatched the phone. "Don't I ever get a day off!"

Kauthar nodded politely as Tasneem walked to the dining area. It was covered with papers likely retrieved from the storage boxes scattered by the table.

"Mom's boss!" Bina plonked herself down on an armchair.

"Oh?" Kauthar said, confused. She had no idea Tasneem worked. In fact, nothing about the Baksh household corresponded with her impression of the family. Her encounters with them were always restricted to the hallways and other common areas. With the exception of a few oversized Quranic plaques on the wall—the kind that could be purchased from any number of stores in Brampton or Thorncliffe—the sparse furnishings, stark walls, and general disarray could not have been less indicative of the pious, haughty neighbour Kauthar had always shied away from. And now this new revelation about *a boss*! How long had she resented Tasneem for being one of *those women* who never had to worry about catching a bus to work in the dead of winter, or having an Indira breathing down her neck when she got there!

Bina ran her fingers vigorously through her wet hair while explaining that her mom worked as a translator for a law firm. Kauthar tried to keep up, not only with all this new information but also with the way Bina talked, like a pukka Canadian, her tongue moving faster than Kashif's. It made her self-conscious about her own stilted

English. And Hassan did most of the talking when they were together. That was why she always liked to have Kashif sit in on her doctor's appointments.

"Yeah, Mom's fluent in six languages, including Arabic, which she learned when we lived in the Gulf. We all speak it—well, everyone except Dad! He can *read* Arabic, though. That's his hasanat."

Kauthar knew the term but couldn't recall what it meant. It had been so long since she'd been to masjid, done namaaz or any other kind of religious observance, her stinging sense of inadequacy around Tasneem creeping over her again.

" 'The one who recites the Quran effortlessly will be in the company of angels. The one who recites with difficulty, stammering or stumbling through its verses, will have twice that reward,' " Bina elaborated. "Or something like that!"

"Bina, what all are you telling our guest?" Tasneem returned, flustered. "And what's taking your sister so long with the chai? Go help her, please!"

Kauthar waved her hand in the air. "Nothing for me! I can't!"

"No tea?"

Kauthar lifted her sweater up since she was only in the company of women, and pointed to the stoma protruding from her stomach. She tried not to tear up. She ached for a cup of tea, but the cancer had denied her the right to eat, to drink, to do the most basic and natural of things without feeling like she was being stabbed by a hundred knives—this seemed like a special kind of punishment, and for sins that must have been so great she just did not know how to atone for them.

"Astaghfirullah!" Tasneem cringed.

"It's a PEG, Mom! A feeding tube!" Banu said, as she entered the room carrying a tray of chai and biscuits.

"Yes, PEG!" Kauthar said, relieved not to have to explain things she herself only barely comprehended.

"I'm very sorry you have to go through all this, Kauthar-bhain. It must be so-so hard." Tasneem set herself down.

Kauthar looked at each of the three women gathered around her: Banu, her hair flattened by the head coverings she had taken off upon entering the house, now sitting across from her in jeans and a sweat-shirt; Bina, with her wet hair slowly drying in loose waves, sitting cross-legged on the armchair in her blue kaftan; and Tasneem, a busy-body who always managed to keep her own affairs tightly guarded, now at such an intimate proximity to her on the sofa, talking to her like a real barri bhain—a big sister! The sight of them peering at her with curiosity and compassion bore into Kauthar's shield.

"It's like my uncle used to say, Tasneem-bhain," Kauthar switched to Urdu, finding English too hard to manage in states of distress. "He used to call anyone strong or powerful a 'Ravi,' like the river. In fact, there was an old Mughal Bara Dari built on the riverbanks, but the Ravi tore up the land around it. We took a boatride to this place for a picnic when I was visiting my cousins in Islamabad. It was like our own special little island, and my uncle explained that it was the river that put it there. It was the river that turned it into an island. But if you saw the Ravi now, all parched and choking, you'd never appreciate the force it once had. That's me, Tasneem-bhain. I'm not the Ravi that once was. I'm the Ravi as it is now: drained and powerless."

"No, Kauthar-bhain, you're wrong! You've survived whatever Allah-mia has asked you to endure. And, mash'allah, you're still standing, like the Bara Dari! You just need to give yourself more credit!"

Kauthar detected something in her peripheral vision. It was Bina holding out a tissue box. Kauthar touched her cheek, shocked by how wet it was. How long had she been crying! She felt her chest heave and release a breathless wail. Then, a slight compression of warmth. It was Tasneem who'd taken her hands in hers. The girls looked on, their own eyes welling up.

"Doctor said not . . . out . . . of . . . woods," Kauthar sputtered through her sobbing. "Maybe I won't make it."

"God is great!" Tasneem assured her. "You will get through this."

"Mom's right, Aunty-ji!" Bina said.

"There are so many medical advances these days," Banu added.

Kauthar tried to straighten herself up and wriggled her hand from Tasneem's. "Zia-bhai will be home soon?" she asked.

"He's out of town right now, but he'll be back just in time for Eid." Then, as a welcome afterthought, Tasneem said, "Will you come to the Eid dinner at the Centre this year, Kauthar-bhain?"

"Mom!" Banu whispered. "The PEG!"

Tasneem scrambled. "I just meant it would be good to get out of the house, hai-na? And even Kashif is going to be there! In fact, I'm sure he'll be helping out with the other volunteers."

"Kashif?"

"Yes, of course! He didn't tell you? Ishaq-bhai really depends on the young volunteers, you know! He thinks very highly of your son! We all do!"

Kauthar was taken aback by how much Tasneem seemed to know about her son's goings-on. Now all those little things she had been noticing in Kashif over the last months were starting to make sense, like the religious words he was using, the kind of people he was talking to on the phone, and all the time he was spending out of the house, outside his working hours at the gas station. Here she thought he was spending time with his father and that gori, when all the time he was going to this big Centre!

"In fact, I'll tell Zia to make arrangements for not one but *two* sheep for qurbani this year!" Tasneem said, still jabbering away. "It will be our extra prayer for your good health."

"You could come for a little while, Aunty," Banu proffered.

"I can drive you back if you want to leave early!" Bina added.

"Yes, yes, beti!" Tasneem sighed. "But remember when your father's home he likes to be the one to drive! Every man likes to be the captain of his own ship!"

"That's so sexist, Mom!" Bina scrunched her face in a way that Kauthar found as unexpected as it was charming. It was enough to let down her guard.

"Yes, I'll come!" she sputtered, unsure if she was heard over the minor squabble erupting between mother and daughter.

"Aunty-ji said she'll come!" Banu cupped her mouth like a loudspeaker.

"It's settled, then!" Bina said coyly. "I'll be Kauthar-Aunty's chauffeur for the night."

"Alhamdulillah!" Tasneem cried, her arms once more extending outward in a perfect V.

17

Marisol predicted her footprints would long have disappeared by the time she got home, the snow an equalizer of space that had little regard for human trespassing.

"It's a bit early for this," she said as they came to the end of the block.

"You've been in Toronto much too long!" Elise countered.

Marisol took this as a personal rebuke. In fact, much of their reunion had felt like a series of pinpricks. Nothing too obvious, nothing too perceptible. But enough to feel bruised by the end of the night. She hadn't counted on their time apart making her so sensitive.

"Speaking of which, I don't think your Toronto friend likes me too much," Elise remarked. "Did you see how tense she was when we were talking about Peru?"

"No." Marisol shoved her hands into her pockets. She had to admit to herself that Elise was right: living in Toronto had made her forget how the cold in Montreal had a different bite.

"Maybe that was because you were just as uncomfortable as she was!"

"You had barely said hello before you got into all that! And since when do we have to broadcast our history?"

"I thought she was your friend. Your new bestie." Elise let a man walking his dog get by, forcing them to rub shoulders. "Anyway, I really don't know why you even bothered to invite me tonight! All you did was take her side on everything. Even those horrible murders."

"I wasn't taking sides!"

"Don't you think it's a bit hypocritical to criticize this society for not being tolerant of other people's beliefs and then be so damn . . . "

They rounded the corner onto avenue de la Croix, taking the long route to Metro Côte Vertu on Elise's urging.

"Go on . . . "

" . . . judgmental!"

"What gave you that impression?"

"Je ne suis pas naif, Marisol! Can't you see she makes you ashamed of us?"

Marisol whipped her hands out of her pockets and blew on them with Malbec-tinged breath. "Don't be so dramatic! And there's no 'us' anymore, remember?"

They kept a safe distance from each other for the last stretch of de la Croix, which was deserted save for a few open stores, including Café Beirut. Music filtered across the street from the café, and Marisol immediately recognized one of her favourite Rai songs, the blend of French and Arabic lyrics a balm against the cold.

"Aïcha, Aïcha, écoutez-moi," she mouthed the words softly.

Elise stopped outside the café. The glass exterior revealed a room filled with older Middle Eastern men sipping tea, playing backgammon or chess, and likely reminiscing about old times.

"Maybe you're in love with her, then!" Elise raised her voice.

"What?"

"Your chère Aïcha—your Aruba, *but not like the island!*"

"Don't be mad!"

Elise grabbed Marisol's hand, forcing them to face each other and pulled her into a wet, demonstrative kiss. Marisol yielded but on catching the stares of their all-male audience, backed away and kept walking, mortified to think her dad and Bassam had been sitting here earlier that day.

She sensed she was walking alone and turned around to find Elise flicking off the men in the café. "That really wasn't cool!" she said, as Elise caught up with her.

"Did you see the way they were looking at us?"

"Who could blame them!"

"That's how *she* was looking at us all night! Like we're circus freaks!"

"You're unbelievable!" Marisol quickened her pace, wishing she'd insisted on taking the short cut.

"Arrête!" Elise called out from under the blue-and-white awning of a Greek restaurant. "Just stop for a minute! S'il te plaît!"

Marisol shrugged and walked back to join Elise under the awning, relieved to be off the slush.

Elise pulled out a joint and proceeded to grapple with the lighter, which kept getting doused by the wind.

"Hey! I thought you'd given up!"

"I had! I have!" Elise shook the lighter. "I just haven't slept since coming back from Uganda. It helps with the jet-lag."

The lighter finally cooperated and Elise took a quick drag before handing it to Marisol. "I went all the way to Africa to get over you, you know that?"

"I didn't realize . . . "

"Well, you wanted the truth, and there it is." Elise inched closer and rubbed their noses together. "I almost forgot how cold you get!"

"That tickles."

"I know. I remember," Elise said, pressing their bodies closer. She slipped a hand under Marisol's coat, groping her way to her breasts. Marisol's nipples hardened and she yielded to another kiss, tasting a strange concoction of cannabis, dolmas, and vanilla lip balm.

"Je t'aime," Elise whispered, her breath hot against Marisol's ear.

"Don't!" Marisol pushed back, dislodging the joint between her icy fingertips. It fell on the ground and extinguished on contact.

"Fuck you!" Elise ran off.

"Wait!"

"I got the message, loud and clear, OK!" Elise shouted, without looking back.

Marisol watched Elise cross the street and disappear into the subway station. She followed after her, but was intercepted by an Evangelical peddling *Atonement-for-our-Sins* brochures. She considered going inside the station, but to do what? To say what? Instead, she bummed a cigarette from an approachable-looking guy standing by the entrance, hoping a smoke would give her fading buzz a reboot. The Evangelical, who had taken ownership of the entrance, shooed the smokers away, and Marisol found herself staring at a *Come In, We're Open* sign blinking through the snowfall. It was the coffee shop from which poor old Bassam and the others were kicked out. The sad picture her dad had painted of the incident compelled her to cross the street.

The store seemed empty, at least from her angle, but she was unable to tear herself away, shuffling in place to stay warm. The friction loosened a brick perched on a construction pile.

Why do all these places look exactly the same? she thought, as she brushed the snow off one of the bricks. Same tables bolted down to the same floors. Same colour schemes and the same glass cases displaying the same damn food, from here to Timbuctoo. What's so special about being the same? she wondered, setting herself a few paces back from the glass exterior. Since when did all this sameness become the recipe for success?

She placed herself at the edge of the sidewalk, her fingers tightening around the hefty object. Would it kill them to try something different?

She felt her heart pounding as she lifted her arm and swung it back, far enough to achieve maximum velocity, when a young black woman appeared from behind the counter, handing an elderly white man his order. They made eye contact and Marisol's arm dropped. The brick hit the ground, disturbing the rest of the pile.

She started to run, the wind hitting her face like glass particles.

By the time she reached her doorstep, cold, wet and winded, the snow had stopped falling, the footprints replaced by a muddy trail of crushed, dampened leaves, just as she had predicted.

18

Arubah would have been content to skip the city tour on such a cold day. That was before she found herself among the festive displays at Marisol's favourite market. It was their first stop, and it hadn't disappointed with its otherworldly season's offerings of knobbly gourds and purple heirloom vegetables, its fresh produce stalls where red chilies hung like crimson chandeliers, and tropical flowers jostled for supremacy against bales of hay and colour-coded chrysanthemums. Arubah was happily assaulted by the sellers' sing-song slogans, *Deux-pour-un! Dernière chance*, as they noshed on seasonal fare or indulged in things like Portuguese egg tarts, arguing about whether chilies were native to the Americas or Asia, Marisol eventually winning out, as usual. They ended up spending far too long at the market, but it was easy to get lost in its maze of stalls and eateries, some managed by a new generation of immigrants and eco-farmers, but most by people whose sun-wrinkled faces and farmer's joual spoke of up to three centuries of toil in the St Lawrence Valley lowlands—land long since wrestled from the Iroquois and developed into commercial farming communities by Jean Talon, whose name the market bore.

"Next stop: Vieux Montreal!" Marisol announced as they got back on the subway to head to the city's Old Port in the historic district.

"You'd be a great tour guide, Marisol!"

"Montreal born and raised! It's in my DNA!"

"I know Toronto well enough, but not like this. Now, the GTA—that's another matter! Ask me where to find the best mithai shop in

Brampton, or the fastest bus route from Rexdale to Richmond, and I'm your woman!"

"You're hilarious."

"Seriously, though. Thanks for showing me around."

They took a break at a boardwalk by the river's edge. Arubah was struck by the power of the Saint Lawrence, whose ancient trajectory they had followed for at least half of their train journey from Toronto.

"For fuck's sake, did you see how she was looking at you!" Marisol cursed after a woman who scowled at Arubah as she passed. "Call me paranoid but things just haven't been the same here lately. Hijab, niqab, beard, turban, brown skin. It's like everything's a target for whatever pent-up resentment's been festering under the ice all along!"

Arubah tasted a drizzle of salt and realized she was tearing up.

"I'm sorry. I didn't mean to upset you."

"Oh, it's not that." Arubah wiped a wet stain from her cheek. This was the perfect opportunity to tell Marisol about *the incident*. She had been meaning to bring it up at the house but after Amin Hamid's news, she hadn't wanted to turn a thunder shower into a hurricane. *One tempest at a time*, her mom always said. She had almost drawn attention to it at one point in the night, but thankfully no one had picked up on it.

"There's something I want to talk to you about," Marisol started, like a mind-reader. "About last night."

"Right, there's something I—"

"It's about Elise."

"Oh," Arubah stopped. "What about her?"

"What did you think of her?"

"She seemed nice. And I thought her missionary work was fascinating, especially her time in the interior—"

"She's not a missionary!" Marisol cut her off sharply. "She's an NGO! She only worked at a missionary chapter as a favour to a colleague, when her contract ended in Lima!"

"All right, already!"

"I'm sorry." Marisol found a bench and sat down. "I guess it's still not easy for me to talk about Peru."

"But it did sound like they were doing good work. Didn't Elise say they were helping people displaced by a mining company?"

"Yeah, sure," Marisol mumbled, staring out at an abandoned silo at the river's edge.

"It sounded horrible—the contamination of the Marañon, and everything."

"Uh, right," Marisol started coming round. "It was a Canadian mining company, you know."

Marisol disappeared into her thoughts again, leaving Arubah to take in the scenery. There was an island in the river with a giant metal sphere at the centre of it. She wanted to ask what it was but her friend was lost to memories of Elise's work with that Chapter. Marisol knew it was a temporary stint but something about that group had raised a red flag. Like why they were stationed at a place that was in dire need of more urgent and practical things, like access to safe drinking water because of the mercury spills, or even protection from armed militias. Elise insisted no one was forcing anyone to give up their beliefs, and wasn't aid in some form better than no aid at all. Back then, they had got off on sparring with each other, their alcohol-fuelled banter just another act of foreplay. She felt sickened by it all now, including her own claims to *real world experience* when really it was more like an extended vacation. Maybe that was why Elise's presence had dredged up all of those same uneasy feelings.

"Did you ever read that poem, 'Take up the White Man's Burden'?"

"Maybe in first year English," Arubah said and slapped her cheek, caught off-guard by a hit of arctic river spray. "Why?"

"It's not important," Marisol stood up decisively. "We should probably get going before you get completely soaked. And we can take a quick walk down rue St Paul on our way. It's worth it."

Rue St Paul really delivered, with its cobblestoned alleys and fleur-de-lys flags flapping in the wind. But Marisol retreated again, leaving

Arubah to fill the silence with talk about her term paper. Isabel had helped her hone in on a topic, recommending she examine citizenship as a shifting construct. "I mean, like the daughters who got killed—they're referred to as *Canadian*. But the older woman, the first wife and victim, she's more or less left nameless, identity-less." Arubah felt her excitement for this line of questioning increase. "And then there's the perpetrator—the father and his current wife—they're referred to as *Muslim*, pure and simple. Almost as if they can't be *Canadian* and accused of *barbaric cultural practices* in the same breath. But all of them are Canadians!"

"Sounds like Mom! Or should I say it sounds like *you*, Future District Attorney Anwar!"

"I don't know why I said anything about law school! I'm really not thinking about it that much. It just came out because of something Elise—"

"What about her?"

"Well, the way she couldn't believe someone *like me* could be in a Women and Gender Studies program! Like I can't be a feminist or something! Like wearing a hijab and thinking for oneself are mutually exclusive!"

"She's not that out of touch, but OK, what else?"

"Nothing. That's it."

Marisol didn't push and they pretended to be absorbed by the impressionist landscapes in the art galleries lining the street, till a café provided an opportunity to get out of the cold.

"That barista reminds me of someone, minus the man bun," Arubah mused, waiting on the tea she had taken far too long selecting from a French menu.

"In one of our classes?"

"No. A guy from the Islamic Cultural Centre. He's been a volunteer there for a while."

"Intriguing!" Marisol drawled.

"You said you're coming to this year's Eid festival, right?"

"Only if I can meet this mystery man of yours!"

"It's not like that!" Arubah said defensively. "He's the son of someone I worked with at Ginetti's. That's how I know him. I feel bad for him, really."

Marisol pushed for more details, and Arubah offered up some gossip about the day she'd seen Kashif's father with another woman, hoping this would throw her friend off the scent. Marisol had the annoying habit of teasing her about her nonexistent love life, as if it were a problem that she took it upon herself *to fix*. Maybe it was just as well she didn't have the chance to bring up Kashif sooner.

"And what is this not-so-mysterious man's name?"

"Kashif."

"Nice! But back up, how do you know his dad?"

"He gave me a lift from the factory once, during a snowstorm. He and Kauthar, Kashif's mom, had insisted on it. He seemed like a nice enough man, but things were definitely kind of tense between them . . . Oh God, was it so awful of me to tell her what I saw! I just figured it was better she knew, and I was worried about those gossipmongers at work."

Arubah drifted back to the day she had tried to talk to Kauthar about her husband. It was the same day she had yelled at Indira, their supervisor. She was lucky she didn't lose her job over it. She remembered being on edge that day, well before she had got to work. For one, she had been wrestling with whether she should tell Kauthar about her cheating husband. And then, juggling her classes, the long commutes and her erratic shifts—it was all too much. She was convinced Indira was going out of her way to make things more difficult for her. She was even considering lodging an official complaint against her, not only because of her own issues but also because she was tired of watching her power-trip over Kauthar and some of the other women. She still couldn't believe how she had taken her old boss to task over their working conditions! It was quite the rush. In retrospect, Arubah wondered if this was the day the law-school bug had taken hold of her. But where was her voice when she most needed it, that day outside the Centre? Why was it so hard for her to defend herself, especially when she hadn't shied away from speaking her mind on the bus! Was it because she just couldn't imagine those teenagers going that far? They had caught her off guard, leaving her mute and helpless. She never wanted to feel that way again.

"It was brave of you to tell her the truth. Not many people would put themselves on the line like that."

"Oh, I don't know about that. It's just that some of Indira's hangers-on were riding poor Kauthar pretty hard already, complaining that she slows down the assembly line. You'd think in a place where the majority of workers are desi women, there'd be less backstabbing and more solidarity."

"So much for *white men saving brown women from brown men*, eh!"

"Sorry?"

"I said sometimes brown women need saving from other brown women!" Marisol laughed.

"Right."

"And what about her son—Kashif? Does *he* know that *you* know?"

"Of course not! Like I said, he's just an acquaintance!" Arubah turned tomato red.

Marisol hand-gestured "I see you" with two fingers. "Seriously, Arubah, maybe it's time to get hitched. I mean, no wedding bells or anything. Just a good old-fashioned boyfriend!"

Here we go again, Arubah sighed.

"God, I hope your mom's not picking out a *suitable boy* from Pakistan for you, is she?"

Arubah hadn't really thought about this, but she could well imagine her grandfather raising the subject of marriage. "My mom wouldn't do that, but . . . "

"But what? Would you actually consider it?"

"I don't know."

"Arubah!"

"Relax! You know I want to finish my degree and see where that takes me before anything else!" Arubah bobbed her tea bag up and down like a fishing bait. "What about you? Do you think you'll ever get married?"

"Don't play dumb, Arubah! I know what you're getting at!"

"What?"

"Just look me in the eye and tell me that if I were to say I'm back with Elise or some other woman, you'd be OK with it. You'd be happy for me."

"Of course, I want you to be happy!"

"Happy but *damned*, right?"

"Why would you say that! It's Elise, isn't it? She thinks I'm a complete nun or something!"

"It's not Elise! It's . . . " Marisol hesitated. "It's *you*! I just don't know where I stand with you—"

"What do you mean?"

"Sometimes you make me feel like only a part of me is good enough. Like the other part is . . . haram."

"You know as well as I do what Quranic teachings have to say on the subject."

"I'm not a *subject*, Arubah. Or a Quranic teaching or even a piece of legislation, for that matter. And FYI, I'm Muslim, too, so yes, I know what those views are. And I also know there are other ways of interpreting them."

"But you don't do namaaz—I mean, you're not a *practicing* Muslim," Arubah objected.

"Ah, there it is! I'm not a *real* Muslim, like *you*! So, I guess it doesn't really matter what I do because I'm already going to hell, right!"

Arubah was about to mention the novel she had found last night. *Ana Hiya Anti.* She wanted to ask if the book was a present from Marisol's dad, because the blurb mentioned it was set in Lebanon. She had read quite a bit of it before falling asleep, and hadn't been prepared for the candor with which it described a lesbian relationship, even though homosexuality was criminalized during that time, under what she assumed to be Islamic laws. It was only when she flipped back to the foreword—a habit of reading every part of a book which her Victorian Lit professor had drilled into her—that she learned these were older laws put in place by the French, under the old colonial regime. She didn't know how to reconcile this revelation with her own assumptions about Muslim countries, and wondered if it would be inappropriate to ask Marisol's dad about it. Then again, would she have had such conversations with her own dad . . .

"Hello? . . . " Marisol's phone interrupted them. "Papa? No, nothing's wrong! Just a little out of breath. We've been walking a lot! . . . Yes, we'll be home soon."

Marisol hung up and relayed her dad's information about a demonstration amassing not far from where they were. He wouldn't have alerted them were it not for the fact that it was organized by a white supremacist group on the law enforcement watch list.

"Apparently, they're arriving in busloads from Quebec City to denounce some immigration policy. But Dad says it's all just a ruse for their more Islamophobic agenda. I think he's being a bit overprotective, but we should probably just call it a day." Marisol slipped her arms into her jacket. "If you're still up for a walk we could take the Metro from the Quartier des Spectacles. It will reduce the number of subway connections home, if nothing else."

Arubah was relieved to escape the brewing argument, but she couldn't walk another step by the time they reached the Quartier des Spectacles, Montreal's entertainment district.

"Shit! How did the demonstration end up here?" Marisol griped. "They must be marching across the city!"

Arubah scanned the mass of bodies covering the entire city block. An occasional chorus of voices erupted from a smaller rag-tag group flanking the east side, while those gathered in the central square, right outside the subway entrance, were formidable not only in number but also in their collective silence. They seemed to be adrift in a sea of fleur-de-lis signs, like the ones in Old Montreal, only these were bigger, bolder, and underscored by an acronym she couldn't make out from where they were standing. The images on the placards were easier to read from a distance—a hammer-and-sickle, gay-pride symbols, and a cartoonish silhouette of a woman in niqab behind bars, all of which were crossed out with a big black X. Groups of protestors also hauled large white banners displaying French slogans that were also easy enough to read: *Non a l'immigration. Aucun compromis. Liberté d'expression! Au nom du peuple!*

The words rang loud in her ears even though the bodies holding them up remained silent, making the group from the opposing side chanting antifascist and antiracist slogans seem all the more belligerent and confrontational. Arubah wished someone would break rank among the silent ones, but they only raised their white banners higher.

"Come on!" Arubah felt a tug at her sleeve. "We'll have to walk a few more blocks but we can take the north side entrance."

Arubah didn't budge, a rolling credit of faces and names flashing through her mind: Dr Mona Ali; Uzma and her daughter Sehr; Amin Hamid's friend Bassam; the nameless victim of the "honour killing" she just couldn't shake; Kashif, Kauthar. Her mom. Her dad. She felt them all watching, as if the next step would be the point of no return.

"No! We're here now. We can cut across!" she said.

"Are you crazy!" Marisol scrutinized Arubah and then the subway entrance, as if both were just beyond reach. "You know the silent protest is just a game, right? It's their sheep's clothing! Things could get ugly in a heartbeat!"

"We can't avoid them," the voice of that other Arubah replied—the one who confronted Indira. The one she didn't think would reappear, at least not after the day she became the target of a hate crime. There: she said it! It was a hate crime! "*I* can't avoid them," she said.

Marisol lifted Arubah's jacket hood over her hijab, and then pulled down the Montreal Canadiens baseball cap over her eyes. "Please, whatever you do, keep your hood on, don't let them see your hijab and for god's sake, don't make eye contact!"

"I promise." Arubah prayed Surah Al-Fatiha, and took the first step.

III

No Cause for Alarm

19

Kashif sat cross-legged in one of the dozens of rows of congregants, many softly reciting "Allahu Akbar," as their fingers moved nimbly over black rosaries. They all sat on the floor, each one perched on his own janamaz, a prayer rug Kashif had nicked from his mom, since she no longer seemed to have any use for it. The Salat al-Eid, the special morning Eid service, was only attended by men, but he took comfort in being part of something that cut across other kinds of differences. In fact, in this grand hall it was easy to picture the billion other Muslims around the world sitting in similar rooms filled with people of all colours, almost as if Islam had written one of the earliest books on "diversity and inclusion"—terms he had come across under the heading, "Sensitivity Training," on the Police Academy website.

Unaccustomed to sitting on his haunches, Kashif eyed the chairs along the hall's perimeter set up for the elderly, disabled or infirm; most of them were empty. He wished the imam would begin the service. Mentally setting himself apart from the fidgety kids around him, he tried to emulate the older men, who sat in quiet reflection and with such purposeful patience, though he had to chuckle at one of the fathers confiscating his kid's cell phone. It made him miss his dad.

Like the elders around him, Kashif had also intended to surrender himself to the experience, but being in such a large mosque on one of the most important days in the Islamic calendar brought up other concerns he could hardly suppress. If there were ever a place where *people gather in the largest numbers*, as the hate-letter had put it, this was it.

In this wide-open space that announced itself like a billboard, weren't they sitting ducks to the people who wished them harm? And what of the hall's shadowy corners—perfect places to bide one's time till the room filled to capacity. Even the congregants themselves weren't off his radar for signs of suspicious behaviour, like a nervous twitch or a hand reaching inside a jacket . . .

Kashif wondered if they'd be any safer in one of the smaller mosques, given what the Masjid Omar Bin Al-Hamad endured, more than once, if Nasser's unofficial reports were to be trusted. But he desperately wanted to experience his first Eid prayer in a real mosque built on the principles of Islamic architecture, not in some depressing room in a grungy commercial plaza. He wanted to pray in the kinds of places he'd seen in his parents' photographs, like the one of his mom outside the Badshahi mosque in Lahore. Or the one in Turkey his dad called "the world's most spectacular mosque," the Hagia Sofia, which he had seen in an old James Bond movie. This was hardly a Badshahi or a Hagia Sofia but it had its own dignity, with its classic dome elevating a centre hall, its arched windows flooding the space with natural light, and five green columns representing the five pillars of Islam, adding to what he could only describe as a place of contrasts: expansive yet inviting, unadorned but striking, grand but humble.

A microphone reverb made Kashif's heart skip a beat, as everyone sprang to their feet at the sight of a youngish-looking man who introduced himself in a distinctly Canadian accent as Imam Ghalib.

"Allahu Akbar," a soothing voice filled the room through a set of loud speakers.

"Allahu Akbar," echoed the voices of young and old now standing shoulder to shoulder, their hands held in front in the prayer gesture, poised to submit to the call of the imam. Kashif had attended Salat al-Juma, the weekly Friday service, enough times to know the difference between a rakat and a takbir, but he still felt like the new kid in school among people for whom such observances were a lifelong practice. He struggled to keep up with the imam's lead, sneaking furtive peaks at

his neighbours, going into the bowing position when they did, standing straight when they did, hands on chest, head turned right, head
turned left. He mouthed the prayer associated with each movement,
careful to mimic the imam's Arabic pronunciation, which was envi-
ably as fluent as his English. Once the awkwardness and hesitation
lifted, Kashif found his stride, his body and mind moving in sync with
the other worshippers.

Bowing as one. Standing as one. Praying as one.

Bismillah ir-Rahman ir-Rahim. The words reached out to him like
a fetal heartbeat. All the fears and anxieties that had weighed on him
since the mosque attack and the assault on Arubah started to lift from
his shoulders. He raised his hands up to recite the Surah Al-Inshirah.
*Have we not expanded your chest, removed from you the burden,
increased your remembrance?* Those things he couldn't seem to control, those things that coloured his life with sadness or anger—his
mom's cancer, his dad's haunting absence—rose to the surface. *Truly,
with every difficulty comes ease,* he repeated among people whose
colour—black, white, brown, and every shade in between—was sus-
pended to the point of irrelevance. *So, when you have been emptied
strive onward, and to your Sustainer turn with longing.* He prayed to
be emptied of these impossible choices. Between mother and father.
Between fathers and sons. Us and Them. East and West. *Saddaqallah
hul Azim. Allah, the Most High speaks the truth.* He rejoiced, buoyed
by the ease with which each prayer now rolled off his tongue. *La Ilaha
Illalahu.* So deep in prayer, he hadn't noticed a new voice blaring
through the loudspeaker.

Imam Ghalib yielded the podium to an older man, informing
the congregation of their venerated guest's credentials and the long
journey he had made from Britain to join them. Sheikh Imam Yusuf
Badawi returned the barest nod of acknowledgement and, without
further ceremony, commenced: "Slaves of Allah! . . . "

Kashif cringed but tried to keep an open mind—each imam had
his own style, after all; and these were just translations, as Ishaq-bhai

always reminded them. Some translations were more in step with the times than others.

"Eid al-Adha has a deep connection with two great prophets: Ibrahim and Muhammad, Peace and blessings be upon them," Sheikh Imam Badawi expounded. "As Ibrahim set the blade on his son," his voice rose to a higher pitch though his head remained cast downward, "so we too must be ready to sacrifice for the Almighty, to protect what is right and pure. So, we too must sacrifice our . . . " The imam's voice trailed off into a litany of "creature comforts" demanding sacrifice, leaving Kashif's mind to stray back to his earlier preoccupations: the shadows, the places to hide—opportunities lurking behind every crack, corner and crevice, to cause maximum harm.

Sheikh Imam Badawi paused to take a sip of water through a silver-haired forest. "In these sinful, heathen lands we have come to occupy, the sacrifice is greatest," he blustered into the microphone.

Kashif didn't know much about these things, but he'd watched enough Westerns to get that "heathen" was a choice insult—the kind the "cowboys" hurled at the "Indians" any chance they got. And a new litany, this time devoted to the innumerable ways the West was the number one "enemy of Islam," pounded the loudspeaker, transporting Kashif to one of the few sermons he had attended with his dad. He was only seven or eight and recalled being bribed with the promise of a blueberry Slurpee on his way home, but his dad stormed out halfway through the sermon. "I didn't put up with this nonsense back home, so I'm sure as hell not going to put up with it in Canada!" Kashif didn't have a chance to get a word in about *the promise*. "You don't ever have to let yourself be filled with such poison—remember that, beta! You don't need these people to find God!" He had to listen to his dad's rant all the way home, and with no blueberry Slurpee to show for it.

Kashif closed his eyes, trying to recapture the lightness and peace he had felt during the Salat al-Eid prayer, belting out an audible sigh when Sheikh Imam Badawi's sermon finally drew to a meandering close.

Imam Ghalib reappeared with a nervous smile: "Uh, yes, as Sheikh Imam Badawi has reminded us so justly, our Prophet Ibrahim—Abraham to our Christian brothers and sisters—was ready to sacrifice what was most sacred and most beloved to him for Allah, the almighty. And, like our Christian brothers and sisters, we honour and praise the Prophet Ibrahim for this most selfless of acts, and share in the message it brings us: that we too must carry the spirit and commitment of sacrifice in our obedience to the Creator."

Kashif braced himself for more of Sheikh Imam Badawi's doom-and-gloom, but Imam Ghalib paused to look at the worshippers and, with regained composure, said, "And let us not forget our commitment is to be charitable; our commitment is to be compassionate; our commitment is to show service to our brothers and sisters, to bring about goodness and love within our communities as well as the greater good, the wider society of which we are a part—this great multicultural land that has given us a home. This country that has given us the freedom to protect and honour our way of life. Where our leaders, including the prime minister himself, send us wishes of Eid Mubarak, and join us in celebrating this most holy occasion."

The mention of the prime minister seemed a bit over the top but Kashif became aware of the man sitting beside him nodding enthusiastically, hanging on to the younger imam's every last word. He tried to gauge other people's reactions, at least those he could see, but profiles of half-frowns or half-smiles were hardly conclusive.

As Imam Ghalib delivered a final prayer, Kashif thought of Ishaq-bhai. Of the numerous public statements he had made about Islam being "a religion of peace and love" in response to the attack on the little mosque. What good was peace and love when their brothers and sisters could not even walk to or from a bus stop without being assaulted? If teenagers could feel emboldened enough to attack Arubah in broad daylight, then what of the damage carried out by those more strategic in their aims, more entrenched in their assumptions, more radicalized by their beliefs? And what use was Imam Ghalib's message of gratitude for this "great multicultural land" when they couldn't get through a day of celebration without expecting the worst?

Was Sheikh Imam Badawi's claim about their vulnerability in the West really so farfetched? But the "evil West" he denounced so harshly was where Kashif was born, where he had his first fumbling attempt at a kiss and where he got his first paycheque. It was where he did all the things kids did around here, like ice-skating at the local arena, and going trick-or-treating, always wearing that same old stupid cowboy outfit. It was where he wanted to settle down some day and where he wanted to make a difference. Like being a cop. Though he wondered if, like that second-hand cowboy outfit his mom bought at the thrift shop, the idea of becoming a cop was another hand-me-down, never a perfect fit. Something always required fixing, like the pants were too short, the hat was too big, or the gloves were too tight. And his mom, who was neither schooled in sewing nor in Halloween, felt her parental duty began and ended with having to spend her hard-earned money on *ye pagal chisen*—such crazy things.

Now that he was thinking of becoming a real cop, could he really see himself wearing one of those uniforms for the rest of his working life, strutting his stuff, and swearing to *serve and protect* in a place where it wasn't always clear *who* was being served and *what* was being protected. If he were called out to a road blockade or standoff like the one Frank described, what would he be protecting exactly, and whose sense of peace would he be required to maintain? Was Frank so sure of who or what he was defending out there? Did he even care, or was he just doing his duty? Didn't he say he wanted that land by the river kept out of the hands of developers, too? But for whose benefit, exactly? His own?

And what about the *who*? At least on this score, he knew where to start. The *who* were the people in this room. People who were tired of feeling like burglars in their own homes, "persons of interest" rather than people with hobbies and achievements and all of the other things that made people . . . interesting. The who were the people who didn't need to have their backs up against the wall 24-7, either because some-one like Sheikh Imam Badawi made them feel like exiles in purgatory, or because of the apologists who conditioned them to keep a low pro-file, making pretty speeches of thanks and gratitude for privileges and rights that others took for granted.

The man to his left patted Kashif on the shoulder and wished him Eid Mubarak, signalling the service had come to an end. As Kashif rolled up his janamaz and waited for the elderly to make their way out of the hall, he caught a rainbow of fractals dancing off the crys-tal chandelier at the dome's centre. Each one had its own distinctive blueprint, just like a snowflake. The angle of light had shifted with the sun, casting arabesque patterns in other parts of the room, almost as if they were standing at the heart of a moving kaleidoscope. His thoughts shifted along with the play of light, colour and movement, turning things over, creating new patterns, arriving at different angles, alternate conclusions.

Maybe Ishaq-bhai's unwillingness to make more of the mosque attack and threats was not just his way of taking the high road, Kashif reasoned. Maybe it was a subversive move against the likes of Sheikh Imam Badawi, a way of putting out other kinds of fires before they got started. He hadn't figured that his message of peace could have been directed as much to those *outside* as to those *within* the community. Whichever way he spun it, wasn't there something cowardly about inaction? And was this their only set of choices, between aggression and passivity?

Kashif retrieved his boots from the shoe racks lined up outside the main hall. He followed a stream of men into the late morning sunshine, imagining each of them heading home to round up their families to visit relatives, or maybe even steal a good nap before the evening festivities. Kashif wished he, too, could head home with such luxuries in mind. For him, the evening festivities were weighed down by a different kind of anticipation. Being part of Nasser's surveillance mission at the Centre. Being the community's eyes and ears. Maybe even its first line of defense.

And then there remained all these unanswered questions. What if something *were* to happen tonight? What if they *did* have to confront the worst-case scenario? How would they react? Which choice would they make: enmity at all costs or turning the other cheek at their own expense?

What was the right path? Was there a righteous path? And was there no middle ground?

20

Marisol struggled to focus on Professor Greenwood's lecture. Most days she was *the keener* in the front seat, typing copious notes, and the first to raise her hand to answer a question. Professor Greenwood flashed her a concerned look, a sign that nothing escaped him in a class with a waiting list as long as the enrollment cap. She understood perfectly the privilege it was to have a seat in his seminar, Indigenous Theory and Research Methods, and couldn't bear a single minute of that privilege being wasted by a distracted mind. But her trip to Montreal was taking up all available space in a brain already overcrowded by mid-term exams, the germinating ideas for several term papers, as well as her work at the Rainbow Centre, where she was responsible for drafting a proposal to foster outreach activities with other student-run societies.

The last item was one reason she had been especially eager to pay attention to today's lecture on "relationality." She was learning the hard way that making connections was a tough sell as far as these other societies were concerned, many of them proving reluctant or unwilling to partner on LGBTQ+ rights and issues.

Marisol's antenna went up when it was clear Professor Greenwood was wrapping up. She straightened her posture and tried to make eye contact to indicate she had been listening.

"Interrelationship," Professor Greenwood concluded, "can apply as much to the spiritual as to the natural. It can involve sacred orientations to time, place and space, as well as knowledge transmission and exchange, where knowledge is, itself, dynamic, fluid and relational."

A final round of questions took up the last ten minutes before Professor Greenwood thanked the class for their contributions, announcing he would be handing back their term paper proposals before everyone left. Marisol slipped a laptop into her backpack and grabbed her jacket, eager to retrieve her proposal. She felt she had come up with a really good topic, with a little help from her mom: she had proposed a comparative study of the water-keeper, a central symbol of water conservation philosophies in Mayan and First Nations contexts.

As she waited her turn, she felt someone's eyes glued on her from behind. She did her best not to turn around, pretty sure she knew who it was. He had tried to corner her into small talk about the course a couple of times but she had become adept at giving him the slip or limiting their contact to the barest exchange, like "Yes, that was a good class," or "You can find the suggested readings online." Then he had managed to get a hold of her contact info but she had made a point of ignoring his emails and texts. She had even stooped to flashing him her Rainbow Centre key card, but either he didn't notice or it didn't diminish his interest. She could have sworn he had started lurking outside her other classes, like that time with Arubah after Professor March's lecture, though she had brushed that incident off as mere coincidence.

That was right before Thanksgiving, Marisol reflected. She had been so looking forward to going home for the long weekend, even more so because she'd been excited to show Arubah around Montreal.

Marisol scrolled through her recent texts. Arubah had sent her several messages in the last few days, asking if she still planned on coming to the Eid celebrations at the Islamic Cultural Centre tonight. She hadn't replied yet. Nor had they hung out since Montreal. In fact, they had barely spoken, even on the train ride home, each of them burying their heads in their books on the pretext they had to study. Since then, they only had one class together and that was taken up with the mid-term for Gender and Social Justice. Marisol had breezed through the exam, never one for taking the time to review, unlike Arubah who was obsessive about these things. Normally, she would have waited for her friend to finish so they could compare notes, but she took off, saying she had to run to another meeting, which wasn't entirely false.

Marisol looked at Arubah's second message providing directions to the Centre. She had fully intended to take part in the Eid celebrations this year. She remembered attending a few of these festivities when she was younger, but by the time she reached puberty her parents took a step back, saying it was up to her to arrive at an informed decision about her own spirituality in her own time, and in her own way.

As it turned out, she wasn't really sure where she needed to go in order *to arrive* at this place of spiritual certainty. Wasn't she already there? Maybe she wasn't what Arubah would call a practicing Muslim, but how many practicing Christians had she ever met? And *they* certainly didn't have to announce their religious leanings to the world, one way or another. Sometimes she resented the fact that Muslims had come to be identified by all these signs and symbols. A hijab. A beard. A black robe. Like their sacred identity was a billboard at the edge of a highway. On the other hand, maybe it was simpler that way—maybe it helped cut through all the ambiguity and bullshit. As if to say, *We are what we are. Deal with it!* But what about women like herself? Weren't there as many, if not more, who didn't wear hijab or some other religious symbol? Even Arubah's mother once commented that she and her friends had never worn hijab, only a dupatta when the occasion called for it, and that it was odd for her to see her own Canadian-born daughter adopt it.

All Marisol could be sure of was what she felt. And she felt now, as she had felt as a little girl going to the mosque with her dad, *at home* in Islam. It was like a cosy blanket in front of a warm, crackling fire. And instinctual. Like a child holding a parent's hand to jump over a puddle. She could try to write a whole dissertation on it but when it came down to it, it was more of a feeling—the kind that washed over you like a rainfall or stayed with you like a powerful dream. And it wasn't just one feeling but a whole rainbow of feelings. Like the way she felt any time she heard the azaan. It wasn't as if the muezzin's call to prayer was a familiar sound in Canada, but even hearing it in movies set in Muslim countries could move her to tears, or make her ache for something she didn't even know she was missing. And then there was the grief she felt when something terrible happened to Muslim people—it didn't matter where in the world. As if they were all part of the same body, sharing the same wound and bearing the same scars. That incident at the Tim Hortons in Montreal was a case in point. Her father's pain for Bassam ran so deep that it could just as well have happened to him, in the same way that her father's pain made it seem like it happened *to her*. It wasn't just a civic response to a social injustice. It was more than this. So much more.

Marisol shuddered, remembering the brick she had come so close to throwing into the coffee shop. If she hadn't seen that woman serving a customer, would she have changed her mind? Would it have made a difference if a white employee was there that night? Did she make these kinds of distinctions—the kind for which she would hold others accountable? Until she worked that out for herself, she wasn't ready to tell anyone about it. Not even her parents. Not even Arubah.

Sometimes she couldn't make sense of it: the pull her Muslim identity had on her. Yet she abhorred organized religion, just like her mom, who provocatively called herself a "devout atheist." Marisol was raised by two people who tended not to rely on others for their moral compass, an aspect of her upbringing she would not relinquish for any level of spiritual certainty. Wasn't all that certainty and dogma at the heart of why things had got a bit derailed with Arubah in Montreal? Weren't all these rules and judgments to blame for the way their friendship was being tested now?

Or maybe Elise was to blame, as if she had accepted her dinner invitation with the sole purpose of sizing up Arubah. And even if she wanted to get back together, she didn't have to behave like a jealous schoolgirl. Marisol couldn't think of anything more ridiculous. Not that she owed Elise an explanation, but her relationship with Arubah wasn't like any other friendship she had, past or present. For one, it had nothing to do with growing up in the same town or liking the same things. They shared something that was harder to pin down: it was more like they just *got* certain things. The "honour-killings" lecture in Professor March's course was the most recent example. They both had similar reactions to the way it was framed, even if they came at it from different angles. And even if they were both completely wrong in their approach to that horrible case, or were being overly sensitive about cases that put Muslims in a bad light, Arubah just got that it was more than a lecture to them, like it was for other students. Because when Professor March said "Muslim-this" or "Muslim-that," she was talking about *them*! Or, at least, people who could be their own mothers or father or sisters or brothers.

But Marisol couldn't let go of the other stuff Elise had picked up on—the stuff *she got* that Arubah didn't get, or chose not to get. The stuff that drove her mad about Arubah! Like the way her friend conveniently excused herself from any event involving the Student Rainbow Centre. The way she had politely feigned interest in Elise's stories about Peru, but had never bothered to ask Marisol about it, not even the next day when they had nothing but time to get into it! She'd never asked about her breakup with Elise, much less how she felt about it. There was this whole part of Marisol's life that lurked like a shadow behind the walls of their friendship. But why did she feel the need to erect those walls around Arubah? She was not one to be boxed in, even resisting an endless parade of labels used to straitjacket *her* sexuality, *her* identity, and yet here she was revealing only *parts* of her life, compartmentalizing herself, like her mom's "butchered turkey," for Arubah's sake!

Marisol read Arubah's latest text. It must have arrived when her phone was on mute during lecture. "You can eat biryani to your heart's content!"

She instinctively started to text back, her stomach growling at the mere prospect of a huge plate of biryani: "Save a plate—"

"Marisol Martinez-Hamid!" the professor called out with characteristic formality, which Marisol attributed to his belief in the spirit and integrity of names.

She left the text unfinished and walked to the front of the class.

Professor Greenwood rubbed his clean-shaven chin. "An intriguing basis of comparison, Marisol!"

"Really?"

"Maybe a tad ambitious for the scope of a term paper."

Marisol had been in Professor Greenwood's course long enough to know that some of his lighter digs were compliments in disguise. "Uh, thanks."

"Oh, don't thank me! Thank the trees you'll be felling and the indigo you'll be spilling to execute this massive undertaking!" Professor Greenwood released the paper theatrically.

"Right!" Marisol smiled, as she heard some impatient grunts from the students still waiting on their papers. "See you next week, Professor."

"Kate Newbury?" Professor Greenwood resumed.

Marisol rolled her work into a cylinder and hastily pushed it into an open pocket in her backpack.

"Alex Petrossian!"

Marisol bolted as soon as she heard the name, making a beeline for her dormitory. She really did want to attend the Eid dinner, especially because it was being held at the Centre Arubah talked up so much. And Eid was hard enough on Arubah without her dad in her life, much less without her mom being around this year, she softened. Maybe all that other stuff that had been weighing on her since Montreal could wait. And she had more than a sneaking suspicion that Arubah had been holding out on her, too. Like about this guy, Kashif. She really hoped he'd be there, if only to give her the chance to tease her about him some more. She loved how easy it was to push Arubah's buttons.

Marisol glanced at her watch. Just enough time to get dressed and call for an Uber.

She swiped the key card at the side entrance of her dorm and stopped to finish off the text: " . . . of biryani for me!"

"Hey, Marisol!" a guy's voice ricocheted through the empty chamber of the concrete stairwell. "Wait up!"

"Hi," she said nonchalantly, walking up a few steps. Did Petrossian live here? She'd never seen him in the co-ed dorms before.

"Got a sec?" Alex released the door.

Marisol heard the metal hinges lock into place, the door securely sealed from the outside world. She stopped on the first-floor landing: "Actually, I'm kind off in a rush."

"You dropped something." Alex approached the stairwell with a rolled-up paper in his hand.

Marisol released the backpack from her shoulders. "Oh, shit!"

Alex ascended a set of steps, and Marisol stepped back, extending an arm to retrieve the paper.

Alex made no attempt to release it. "The prof seemed to like it. But you always do so great in his class."

"Uh, thanks."

"Maybe you could give me some pointers. My grades suck this term."

"I like the subject, I guess. Look, I really do have to be somewhere, so—"

"I just figured you wouldn't want to lose the prof's feedback." He unrolled the paper, which was now creased in several parts, and read aloud: "*An ambitious but intriguing premise. The foundation of a fine research paper, and an even finer thesis proposal, if grad school is on your radar.*"

"Hey, that's my work! It's private!"

Alex rolled the paper back into a cylinder and tapped it against the railing. "Must be nice to have professors looking out for you. Sounds like he wants to be your advisor. Or maybe more."

Marisol made a grab for the paper but Alex held it above his head, just out of reach.

"Not so fast! Don't I get a reward? Like the paper for a date?"

"Look, asshole, are you going to give it to me or not!"

Marisol made a second grab for the paper. Alex released it but caught the end of her coat before she had a chance to start up the stairs.

"What the fuck!" she shrieked, and rested a hand on the railing for support.

Alex cupped his hand over hers. "You don't even have the time to say 'Thank you, Alex'?"

Marisol tugged on her hand but he applied more pressure, pinning her down.

"Thank you, *Alex!*" she said through a clenched jaw. "Now let go of me or I'll call Campus Security!" She withdrew her phone with her free hand but Alex hit the back of her arm, catapulting the phone into the stairwell.

"You broke it!" she yelled, looking for a way out. Each floor had its own digital code, an extra security measure since a recent surge of break-ins. The only way out was her own dorm-room floor, several flights up.

"It feels pretty crappy, doesn't it?"

"I don't know what the hell you're talking about!" Marisol tilted her head away. He was so close she could almost taste the coffee on his breath.

"You didn't have to ignore me. You could have had the decency to *just say no! No, thank you, Alex!*" Alex lifted his hand as if he was about to release her, but swiftly caught her by the wrist and twisted her arm behind her back.

Her scream was cut off by a bicep pressed hard against her throat.

"Maybe it's Greenwood you're in such a rush to see!"

"You're choking me!"

Alex hitched his right foot against her boot, and pushed her against the railing. Her head bobbed over the edge like a marionette and she stared into the hollow stairwell, feeling the blood drain out of her cheeks.

"Help!" Marisol's voice ricocheted off the walls, an icy draft suddenly touching her in places where she should have been clothed, and then something cold and sharp, like a belt buckle, dug into her flesh.

"Please!" She tried to kick back at his legs but the more she resisted the deeper his hands drilled into her waist, keeping her immobilized. She tried to remember something, anything, she had learned in the special taskforce meetings, wishing she had taken the self-defense classes she had worked so hard at encouraging her Society members to sign up for.

She squeezed her eyes shut, a last line of defense against the weight of his body jammed up against hers. She was overcome by the pressure till a mere ripple of a sound, like a couple of musical beats, broke through the ringing in her ears. It was the raindrop app she'd picked for her text-alerts. Alex heard it too and shifted his leg, giving her just enough room to hook her fingertips through the backpack lying on the floor. It was weighed down by her laptop but she managed to swing it behind her. It missed the target but Alex's grip loosened, and she seized the bag with both hands before swinging it round again. A crack and then a deep, primal moan ripped through the stairwell as Alex staggered back.

Marisol scrambled up the stairs on Jello legs but soon found her stride, bounding up several steps at a time. Her heart sank when she realized she had missed her floor, knowing she had to take her chances and backtrack if she had any hope of getting away.

"Come on, come on, come on!" Her hand trembled as she entered the code to her dorm room floor. It took several more attempts before she realized she was using the wrong pin number for the security system.

"You almost took my eye out, you bitch!" A voice lashed out at her from below.

The buzzer sounded and released the door. She flung herself inside and collapsed against it, cradling herself in an upright fetal position, her head falling into a cocoon of darkness.

She flinched and threw out her arm defensively when she sensed someone approach.

"Whatever!" a girl who had come out of one of the washrooms sneered.

"Call the police!" Marisol sobbed.

When the girl made no sign of taking her seriously, Marisol must have shot her a look so intense the girl almost fell back.

"Call 911! Now!"

21

Kashif and Arubah stepped aside for a large family, the man decked out in a starched shalwar suit, the woman in a brightly sequined sari, and the kids sporting neon-coloured sneakers or shiny patent leather shoes, no doubt received as Eid gifts.

Kashif had hovered around the main entrance in the hope of meeting up with Arubah *by chance*, and she didn't seem to mind the company. In fact, he was embarrassed by the number of times she apologized for not finding a way to thank him for the earring, saying midterm exams and a Thanksgiving trip had kept her away from the Centre.

"Ugh! Where is she!" Kashif heard Arubah mumble.

"Sorry?"

"My friend, Marisol! I'm still not even a hundred percent sure she's coming!"

"Where does she live?"

"Downtown. In residence."

"That's quite a trek, and there's always so much traffic."

"Yeah, I suppose," Arubah shrugged, watching the family make their way to the dining hall. "What about your mom? Is she here yet? I'd love to say hi."

Kashif silently thanked *this friend*, Marisol, for her tardiness, his nerves settled by Arubah's presence on a day that his mind was otherwise hijacked by what Nasser had set in motion.

Even though he had agreed to be part of the plan, he still had his doubts. What if there was an attack, for real? And what if it was something major, like that mass shooting in Germany or the attack in Switzerland against an Islamic Cultural Centre just like theirs? What were they supposed to do, then? At least his talk with Frank had given him the courage to approach Ishaq-bhai about the letter, but the imam had only repeated his usual mantra: "Kashif-bhai, there is no cause for alarm. There is no doubt the incident at the mosque was designed to arouse tension and fear, but we cannot allow our houses of worship to be filled with anything but peace. People must feel they're coming to a sanctuary, not a gated community."

Kashif had almost snapped on hearing that phrase. No cause for alarm. It was getting old and left a bad aftertaste, like stale chewing gum.

He scanned the parking lot grounds, its empty spaces filling up with more and more cars, more and more families, all of them assuming that the Centre was exactly as Ishaq-bhai described it. A place of peace. A sanctuary. But what if something terrible was being planned against them? Didn't they have a right to know? Didn't they have the right to decide whether they wanted to take the risk of bringing their children to a place marked for an attack, however unlikely, however small?

"Hey, it's your mom!" Arubah shrieked.

Kashif could hardly recognize his mom as she approached the entrance, a soft, chiffon dupatta draped over her head instead of that withered toque, and in an emerald-green embroidered shalwar-kameez which he had never seen her wear before. Nor had he seen her so relaxed and comfortable with Tasneem Aunty, who was accompanying her. In fact, he hadn't taken her seriously when she said she'd be coming not just with Tasneem Aunty but with the whole Baksh family, including the daughters Kashif had only ever known as the niqabi girls who'd sometimes drop by, staying for the brief seconds it took to say "Salaam" and hand over a care package for his mom. Now here she was, all smiles, flanked on each side by Tasneem Aunty and one of her twins. He only wished it was his dad's arm that she was holding on to. Would they ever be a family again? He'd even be OK with an unofficial sort of togetherness, like a blended family. It was enough to make him reconsider breaking the standoff and calling his dad. Especially today. On Eid.

"Ah, there's Kashif!" Tasneem led her entourage toward Kashif and Arubah. "I told you he'd be looking out for you, Kauthar-bhain. He's such a good boy!"

Kauthar acknowledged Tasneem's praise but her warm smile of recognition was directed at Arubah.

"Salaam, Aunty-ji!" Arubah rushed to greet her. "I am so glad you're here! It's been so long!"

When Kauthar finally released Arubah from an epic bear hug and they were all caught up, Arubah inquired if Tasneem Aunty was the same Tasneem Baksh who made those brilliant translations for Dr Ali's Tariq al-Nur campaign.

"Ha, ji!" Tasneem grinned proudly, though half her attention was taken up with a scrutiny of the main entrance. "Arré, where's that father and sister of yours!" she muttered to one of her daughters.

"Probably still squabbling over who's the better driver!" Banu laughed.

"There they are!" Tasneem waved a tissue like the flag-bearer at NASCAR, and then instructed Banu to go on ahead and find them a row of seats together in the banquet hall. She turned and pressed Kauthar's hand affectionately, indicating it was time to follow Banu inside. Kauthar hesitated to go without Kashif and Arubah, till the latter explained she was waiting for a friend and would come in later.

"Mind if I hang out with you guys?" Bina, who had just arrived with her father, asked.

"You also stay, Kashif!" Kauthar instructed. "Wait with Arubah."

Kashif didn't protest, thrilled to have more time with Arubah, even with Bina playing kebab-me-haddi, one of his dad's colourful expressions for *three's a crowd*.

"So, are you guys, like, family?" Bina pried, since she hadn't been around for the earlier round of introductions.

Arubah filled her in on her time at Ginetti's, as a young girl approached them with a tray of pink drinks that matched her garishly pink gharara suit.

"Would you like a sharbat?" the girl asked, her entire face contorted in the act of keeping the drinks from falling off the tray as her mother prodded her along.

Bina carefully picked up a glass of the sharbat. "She's so cute!"

"You'll have one as cute some day," Arubah said.

"Who, me!" Bina almost choked on her sharbat. "That's way, way off!"

"Sorry!"

"No worries," Bina said. "I get it all the time. Like that's my only mission in life."

"No! That's not what I meant!" Arubah replied. "I just meant it would be nice to have kids some day. Though I'm with you one hundred percent on the way-way-off thing!"

Kashif wasn't sure if he should stay or go, finding all this baby talk a bit mortifying. He resolved to try to change the subject when Bina saved him: "I plan on getting my pilot's license. That's my number-one priority!"

"A pilot's license!" Kashif and Arubah broke out simultaneously and blushed.

"Yup!" Bina seemed to catch on to their flirtation and laughed. "I did some flying in Saudi in one of my friend's private Cessnas. We used to live in Saudi before we immigrated here, you know. I even drove a race car there once!"

"But I thought women were banned from driving there," Kashif said.

"A lot of things are banned. It doesn't stop anyone from doing them!"

Kashif waited to hear more about Bina's pilot's license, when he was distracted by a couple making a grand entrance, if only because they were a mismatch made in the bizarro world. Then Kashif saw Kamal, the nice guy whose father owned Al's Roti Hut, walking a few steps behind the couple, and he made the connection: the woman must be Farida, Kamal's sister. When the mystery guy stepped out of the Bollywood-ambit of Farida, Kashif immediately recognized Jamshed, or Jam, the surly guy with the dragon tattoo, whom Nasser had dragged to their meeting. It confirmed a hunch: these two were already an item, and maybe that was why Jam had deigned to meet them at Al's that day. Something about the guy just rubbed Kashif the wrong way.

Much to Kashif's relief, Jam and Farida didn't recognize him, but Kamal, who had found his way to Zafar and the other guys, waved him over.

"Kashif beta," Tasneem Aunty called out just as he signalled to Kamal that he was on his way. She was walking slowly toward him, arm in arm with his mother. "Your ammi had a bit of a dizzy spell. I think she's changed her mind about staying."

"Mom?"

"Hanh, beta," Kauthar said weakly, "I want to go home."

"Maybe too many people. She seems overwhelmed by it all," Tasneem Aunty whispered to Kashif.

Kashif wasn't sure what to do. Part of him was relieved to get his mother back home. Her presence made the whole operation that he and the other guys had planned for the evening more complicated. The other part of him wanted to tell Arubah and the whole Baksh family to leave as well, but they would just think him mad, considering that all of the Eid events, not just here but around the country, had so far transpired, as Ishaq-bhai would say, *without incident.*

Arubah helped Kauthar with her coat, giving Kashif time to check in with the guys. They obviously wanted a chance to go over the plan, even though they had been over it a hundred times by now, and it wasn't that elaborate. The five of them—everyone who'd been at Al's

Roti Hut that day, except Jam and Nasser's younger cousin Arif—
were to be stationed at different strategic points in and around the
Centre. They were all to make an appearance at dinner with their
families and then take up their posts—one on the roof, two patrolling
the unattended areas like the athletic wing, and two to walk around
the grounds in staggered shifts—so there was always someone on the
lookout. Kashif was supposed to take up the first outdoor shift. Now
what was he supposed to do?

Bina, who had disappeared into the banquet hall, returned with a
set of car keys which she held up like a trophy. "I can drive you guys
home!"

"Uh, thanks, Bina! I really appreciate it," Kashif said, unsettled by
the people gathered around him, who looked as if they were in freeze-
frame mode—his mom all hollow-cheeked and pale; Arubah preoccupied by her no-show friend; Tasneem Aunty and Bina; and then
Nasser, Zafar, Kamal and the others eyeing him from across the hall—
and only he had the power to reanimate them.

"Do you want to come with us?" he heard Bina ask Arubah.

"I wish I could, but I really need to wait for my friend," Arubah
sighed. "I'll be here when you get back, though."

Kashif could have sworn Arubah looked straight at him when she
said that. Like the assurance was meant for him. It was exactly the
motivation he needed to stop dithering and take action. It was enough
to hit *play*.

22

Arubah put aside her plate of half-eaten biryani as soon as she got Isabel Martinez's call. Later she couldn't even remember how she had the presence of mind to tell one of those twins something about the nature of the emergency. It certainly hadn't been for their benefit. It was Kashif she had wanted to inform. And for some reason Kashif was her last thought before she got into the taxi. She berated herself for it. After all, Marisol should have been the only person on her mind. And she was! She just wished he'd been there when she got the call. He had left so suddenly. She was worried about Kauthar, too. She had looked so fragile and gaunt. Had Kashif even made it back to the Centre? She had a feeling in the pit of her stomach that she should stay. That she was needed there, too.

"You can eat biryani to your heart's content." Arubah read her earlier text to Marisol, as if that could help erase the last few hours and take her back to the moment Marisol would have been picking out her Eid outfit—like a Moroccan Kaftan with leather pants and knee-high boots—just like her, classic and edgy. To the moment when Marisol would have said she was on her way.

"Save a plate," Arubah read the first text in Marisol's disjointed reply. Her friend had been on her mind all day. Marisol had seemed excited enough about Eid on their train ride back. It was the only thing they had discussed with any enthusiasm—that and their intrepid walk through the big bad wolves at the demonstration. It had felt like a death-defying feat, weaving through those rows of white faces dressed in black, from head to toe. At one point she had felt her hood get dislodged, and she mentally prepared herself for something far worse than a tug at her hijab by a teenager on a dare. Some of the burlier, bearded men looked like they could snap Marisol and Arubah in two with the mere flick of a wrist. And who would be any the wiser, in the thick of that crowd? Now she felt foolish for fancying herself a gladiator in a coliseum, though she had to remind herself that gladiators were despised slaves in Roman times, and she had done nothing more spectacular than walk through a crowd to get to a subway station.

" . . . of biryani for me." Arubah read the second part of Marisol's text—the one that had arrived with a delay of about thirty minutes. It had given her thirty long minutes to curse Marisol for taking so long to get back to her, and for giving her the silent treatment since Montreal. But the truth of it was that she had also been feeling sorry for herself. As much as she had loved being with Marisol for Thanksgiving, she'd be lying if she said she wasn't just a bit envious of the Martinez-Hamid family. She and her mom had been a *family of two* for so long she had never really imagined that things could be different, and her mom had never considered remarrying. Of course, she would have done anything to bring her dad back into their lives but that was more like wanting to turn back time—to bring the rabbit back out of the magician's hat. But with Marisol's family she had come away with a snapshot of a life for which there was no other prototype. She couldn't quite put her finger on it, but it had more to do with an unwritten future than a past she hoped to recover.

How could she have been so selfish, Arubah brooded. Here she was throwing herself a pity-party, when in those same thirty minutes Marisol was . . . she couldn't even get herself to say it. Isabel hadn't given her too many details, leaving Arubah to latch onto empty soundbites, like the digital feed in the subway car. *Assault. Police. Badly hurt.*

Even when she arrived at Emergency and saw medical staff and a police officer hovering around Marisol, the scene in her mind still played itself out like a movie. It was only when she was allowed to enter the curtained-off room and see the massive bruise on Marisol's neck from the chokehold "the assailant" had her in, and her arm in a sling from the injury to her shoulder, that Isabel's garbled message attached itself to an external reality: *She's been assaulted. She's badly hurt. The police are taking her statement. Please, can you go to the hospital and stay with her till we get there? We're taking the first flight out.*

Arubah finally registered the words but she was not prepared to see. Not this. Not Marisol, her beautiful firecracker of a friend, her rock, her sister, all crumpled up into herself like a wad of discarded tissue. She would have sat with her on the edge of that steel-framed cot for days, weeks, months, years—whatever it took. But they weren't alone. A police officer politely asked her to step out of the room, saying she needed to go over the last few details of the victim statement.

Arubah wished she were a lawyer already, just so she could object to the term: *victim statement*. All that time Marisol spent providing students a safe space at the Rainbow Centre. All the ways she fought back for others. For herself. Marisol was nobody's victim.

The police officer must have seen Arubah's distress when she came back out of the room. "You have a very brave friend."

"The bravest." Arubah rummaged through her purse for a tissue.

"Are you going to be all right, Miss . . . ?"

"Arubah. Arubah Anwar. We're friends from uni."

"Well, your friend is going to need your support."

"Do you know who . . . did this?" Arubah teared up. Was he a student in one of Marisol's courses? Did she know him from res life? Did he live in her dorm? Or did he just walk off the streets?

"I'm sorry, but I can't reveal that information. And your friend—well, I wouldn't push her on it right now. And there is a chance she won't want to speak about it at all."

"Of course. I understand. Thank you . . . Officer Barnes." Arubah read the crest on the officer's upper right sleeve: Nekeisha Barnes, OPP Sixth Division. Despite the frantic energy of the Emergency ward, Arubah found herself studying the person beneath the uniform—chocolate-brown eyes, unadorned lips, black hair slicked back, and an imposing frame that didn't quite correspond to the laugh lines around her eyes.

"That cool police officer says you're very brave, but I already knew that," Arubah said when she was allowed back in.

"She's wrong about that." Marisol tried to manoeuvre herself off the gurney. "I should have read the signs!"

"Hey! Hey!" Arubah wedged herself between the gurney and the floor, like an island.

"I should have known better! I should know how to handle a guy like—"

"But you did! I don't think I could have done what you did! I *know* I couldn't . . . " Arubah still hadn't told Marisol about what had happened to her, every missed opportunity seeming to turn a bite-sized omission into a full-blown lie.

"I had so many chances to tell him to back off, but I didn't!" Marisol said with shallow breaths. "So many chances . . . "

Arubah tried not to press for details, as Nekeisha Barnes had advised, but her mind kept conjuring mugshots of possible assailants. Like the guys Arubah caught drooling over Marisol. Or that guy waving at them after Professor March's class. Could it be?

A nurse breezed into the room with two white pills and a paper cup. "This is to help with the pain, dear. It might make you a little drowsy."

"No! I don't want to sleep!"

Arubah draped a flimsy blanket over Marisol's trembling figure, then carefully perched herself at the edge of the gurney. "Officer Barnes said she'll be right outside. She's not going anywhere. None of us are, I promise!"

The nurse checked Marisol's pulse. "That's right, dear. You're safe here."

"It's not that!" Marisol grimaced as she fell back into the pillow. "I just want my damn backpack! Where is it?"

"The police must have it. I can check for you." Arubah slipped off the gurney, relieved to have a mission that could make her feel useful.

She assumed Marisol was concerned about her laptop which contained all of her term papers and course-notes.

"I hit him with it, Arubah!" Marisol said with increased agitation. "I hit him really hard!"

Arubah stopped, wondering if she should fetch Officer Barnes.

"And my phone! Where's my phone!"

"I'll make sure I get everything back for you, OK?" Arubah said, realizing she was making promises she wasn't in any position to keep. If the police had the backpack, maybe they were treating it as evidence, but the assurance seemed to do the trick and Marisol relaxed just enough to let the painkillers kick in.

" . . . Some Eid, huh!" Marisol said groggily.

"Some Eid!" Arubah sighed, suddenly wishing she could curl up beside Marisol and fall into a deep sleep of forgetting.

"Did you text me?" Marisol asked, her speech increasingly slurred.

"Sorry?"

"Someone texted me . . . when he . . . in the stairwell."

Arubah wished she could piece things together for her friend. All she knew was that she was assaulted on campus—a campus that was supposed to have ratched up its security because of the spate of break-ins and assaults. What good was all that extra security now! What had it done to protect her best friend?

"I had given up . . . I didn't know what else to do, then I . . . I don't know . . . I heard water . . . like rain." Marisol drifted in and out. "Did it rain today?"

"No, it snowed," Arubah said, wondering why hospital rooms were always so cold and there were never enough blankets. She retrieved her Kashmiri shawl from her totebag. "It's the first big storm of the season. Just the way you like it!" she said, draping the shawl over Marisol.

Marisol hoisted the shawl up to her neck and inhaled. "Hey, this reeks of biryani."

"Yeah, I guess it does." Arubah recalled the lightning speed with which she had grabbed her stuff and left the Centre. It was a wonder she hadn't knocked over a few chairs and banquet tables in the process.

"Weren't you saving me a plate?" Marisol's head lifted off the pillow.

"Are you kidding! I saved you a whole pot!"

"Does this mean you . . . forgive me?"

"Forgive you? For what!"

"For being a jerk . . . since Montreal."

Arubah felt a stain of tears. She had been trying so hard to keep it together. "Don't be silly!" she forced a smile.

"But I've been avoiding you . . . There! I said it!"

"That's not important. I'm here now." Arubah took her friend's hand. "And your mom and dad will be here soon, too, I promise."

Arubah longed to tell Marisol everything that had been gnawing at her since they'd got back from Montreal. That Marisol's relationship with Elise *had* made her uncomfortable. That she had convinced herself it was Elise she didn't like much but, in truth, it was the *girlfriend-part* she had trouble with. But that was before. Before, when being on the right side of every argument that had to do with Islam seemed more important than being a friend. She still had to work out how to curb those impulses, but she was beginning to ascertain where they came from. It had something to do with her dad. As if she was trying to be *his* version of an ideal daughter. And an ideal Muslim. But she was so busy trying to live up to something no one had forced on her that she forgot that there was more than one way to be Muslim. Amin Hamid was proof of that, but then so was her mom! She was so focused on her dad and what he may have been like or what he may have wanted that she had lost sight of her mom, who always lived her life on her own terms.

Marisol was still shivering so Arubah removed her parka and draped it over the blanket and shawl.

"I'm sorry, Arubah," Marisol said, her head dropping to the side, as if she was seconds away from falling asleep.

"No, I'm sorry, Marisol! I'm so, so sorry!" The words poured out of her like that mountain Marisol had described—the one whose name had something to do with mothers and origins and water.

23

Kashif took the short bus ride back to the Centre, not wanting to hold up Bina. He had felt he needed to stay with his mom long enough to make sure she would be all right alone. The excursion to the Centre, however short-lived, had wiped her out but she seemed the happier for it. He hadn't seen her smile like that since before the treatments—since forever, he realized. She had even gone to bed singing some song. It wasn't in Urdu. That much he could tell. All he could make out was Ravi-this and Ravi-that in the refrain. It sounded like a line from some of the old Punjabi films she liked to watch. It had sounded cheerful, and that was enough to assure him that her outing had not been in vain.

The dining hall at the Centre was still packed by the time he got back. The children had abandoned their seats, giddy on a sugar rush or the sheer thrill of being in each other's company. They zipped around the tables, absorbed in whatever imaginary games the festively decorated hall provided.

Nasser had already gone over the count of projected attendees but nothing had prepared Kashif for the warmth of feeling generated by hundreds of people sharing a meal together. He had never experienced anything like it, figuring this was the biggest shindig he had attended—far bigger than his high school prom or some distant relative's wedding. Neither of those events had held too much appeal at the time, not like this. He had been looking forward to Eid night for weeks. And now, standing in the middle of the banquet hall, at the centre of things, it all made sense. He needed to be here. To see this. To be part of something that eclipsed all those depressing images of Muslims on TV. To be out of the shadow of black-hooded men wielding AK-47s and messages of doom. To see children playing with tinsel streamers and balloons, instead of standing destitute and abandoned in cities destroyed by drone attacks and suicide bombers.

At first, he had just gone along with Nasser's initiative, but now he was all in. Didn't all these people deserve protection? What was wrong about being vigilant? They were not planning on breaking any laws. There was no law against being realistic about how vulnerable their community was to ridicule, to insult, to assault. And if one of them got hurt in the process, then so be it! In fact, wasn't that what being a cop was all about? Or maybe it was just a matter of sacrifice. If it weren't a risk he was willing to take for his own community—for Arubah, for Zafar, for his neighbours, and tonight, even for his mom, whose presence had made the thought of anyone planning an attack that much more horrific—then what good would he be to anyone else?

Kashif caught someone waving at him from across the hall by the buffet tables. He couldn't make out who she was from this distance, and especially through the crowds. That said, there weren't too many women in full niqab, but it was only when the woman held up a set of car keys and mimed holding a steering wheel that Kashif eased up and waved back.

"Hey! You're back!" Bina smiled, helping herself to a big serving of kheer. "How's your mom, by the way?"

"She's OK. Just tired out, I guess. She went to sleep before I left."

"I hope it wasn't a mistake to convince her to come."

"No, she loved being here. Even just dressing up and being with you guys."

Bina started to hand Kashif a bowl for dessert, then pulled back. "I forgot you haven't even eaten dinner yet! You must be starved!"

Kashif swallowed hard as he surveyed the rainbow-coloured dessert buffet—so many sweets stacked up in pyramids of sunflower yellows, carrot-oranges, pistachio-greens, and condensed milk-whites, alongside vessels of syrupy vermicelli, and even a barrel of kulfi ice cream popsicles for the kids. And he hadn't even got to the main courses yet, though he was close enough to inhale the unmistakable aroma of saffron-scented biryani, the goat curry he'd been craving for weeks, as well as trays stacked with a variety of kebab. His dad would have salivated over the kebab platter. They were his favourite.

"Listen, I have a message for you!" Bina shouted, as she moved away from the dessert tables.

Kashif reluctantly followed her. He had hoped he could at least shovel back a plate of goat curry and biryani before joining up with Nasser and the other guys.

"It's from your *friend*, Arubah." Bina winked. "She told us to tell you she had an emergency."

Kashif's heart sank as Bina filled him in on the little she knew, assuring him that Arubah was fine; it had something to do with that friend she was waiting for. A jumble of details ensued over the din of the crowd, including something about hospitals and police. "Anyway, sorry I can't be more specific. She left in quite a hurry, but she did seem eager for you to get the message."

Kashif thanked Bina for the information and found a quiet spot, determined to locate Arubah's number before realizing he didn't know her last name. He considered asking Ishaq-bhai but Nasser had made them swear to keep their contact with Ishaq-bhai to a minimum during Eid night. Coming up short on all fronts, he was about to stash his phone away when he noticed a message in voicemail.

He hoped it was Arubah.

"Kashif, it's Dad! Just Dad calling to say Eid Mubarak. Eid Mubarak, beta."

Kashif repeated the message several times, overcome by the sound of his dad's voice. Then he noticed a second message. "I love you, son. That's all. Eid Mubarak."

Instinctually he hit "reply" and, before he could change his mind, the phone was already auto-dialing his dad's number.

"Kashif?"

"Dad!"

"You got my message?"

"Yes!" Kashif air-fisted his head for hitting reply! Tonight of all nights, when he had to keep it together.

"Beta, are you still there?"

"Yes, Dad."

"It's so good to hear your voice, beta. I've been thinking about you and your mom a lot, especially today."

"How can you say that!" Kashif's firewall was back up. "I mean, why haven't you thought about her while she's been in chemo!"

"I don't understand! Who's getting chemo?"

"Ammi! Who else!"

"Why?"

"What do you mean—why! Why do people get chemo!"

"But she didn't say a word! Why wouldn't she have told me . . . ?" Kashif heard his dad release a torrential sigh, as if the news was only just sinking in. "Astaghfirullah! She really has cancer? For how long? What type? How bad is it?"

"Mouth cancer. And it's pretty bad."

"It can't be!"

Kashif could see Nasser heading his way, no doubt eager for him to take up his post for the night.

"Look, Dad, I really can't get into this now. I've got somewhere to be, but I—"

"Is your mom with you now?"

"No, she's home."

"Achha."

"She's resting. She shouldn't be disturbed!" Kashif blurted out, hoping he hadn't set something in motion that his mom wasn't prepared for—or, worse, something she was in no state to handle.

"Of course, I understand."

Nasser was impatiently pointing to his watch.

"Dad, I really have to go, but I'll call you tomorrow—"

"Do you promise?"

"Yes."

"Then let me promise you something also, beta." Kashif could hear his dad's voice falter. "I promise I'll make things right."

"Sure, Dad." Kashif hung up before he said anything else he might regret, like the fact that his mom's cancer was one of those things you couldn't just make right. He knew this better than anyone, because when he prayed it was always for his mom. Only, so far, it seemed that no one was listening.

IV

A River in Paradise

24

Frank feels water, ice-cold, underfoot. It's murky, like the bottom of a river. Is he fishing? Out at the GR? Where's his gear?

The water's climbing. Up to his shins. He paws at the darkness. Takes a cautious step.

Why can't he feel the slimy river stones under his feet? Why can't he hear the water murmuring through the red willow roots clinging to the banks, or the low-lying buzz of the Jesus bugs walking on the water's surface?

Frank looks up and blinks, hoping it will help clear things up, but he's blinded by a piercing shaft of light.

"Frank!" somebody shouts. A woman.

Cheryl?

Knee-deep now, Frank wades through the water, alarmed by its resistance.

He stubs his toe on something hard and angular. "What the . . . ?" It feels like the edge of a table. He looks up again and sees an old brass chandelier. Just like the one in his living room. There's an undulating wall beyond it. The drapes? They're shutting out the light, just the way Cheryl likes it . . .

"Frank!"

"Cheryl?" Frank turns. His feet give way to a bottomless floor.

What the hell is happening?

"Frank! Get out of the way!" Cheryl screams in time enough for him to see an oak-stained hutch barreling toward him on its side. He dives into the water with no way of gauging its icy depths.

Under the surface objects collide, pipes burst and windows shatter in a liquid echo chamber. He swears he sees a pick-up truck careening past their living room window. It's enough of a shock to propel him back up for air.

"Help!" a muffled voice calls out again.

"Cheryl? Is that you? Call my name again!"

Frank tries to keep himself afloat as he hears the cracking of a whip, like lightning tearing through the trees.

"Cheryl!" Frank screams, swallowing water.

"Frank!" a weakened voice calls back, an arm and then a head appear, barely visible above the surface.

"Oh, Christ! Hang on! For the love of God, hang on!"

Frank pitches himself toward her but something tears into his leg, the heat from the pain discernible even through the glacial water. A slew of objects, large and small, eddy around him like grains of sugar in a teacup. He catches sight of something shiny among the vortex of debris, convinced he sees a heart and then a shimmering tail trail after it. He needs to save it before it sinks, he thinks, and hooks a finger through the chain, a silver locket coming to rest against his palm.

When he resurfaces the water settles into a rhythmic lapping. Like a shoreline on a perfect summer's day. He dips a hand into the water, his feet, bone-dry, and planted on the ground. On solid ground.

Not quite.

It's shifting back and forth, an exacting scale of movement, like a swinging pendulum.

He looks below and finds himself seated on a narrow plank extending across a half-shell. A concave cradle. Like the hull of a small boat. Like the ones he'd take out to do a spot of fishing.

He yields to the gentler current, lulled into a state of peace by the symphony of reeds and cattails blowing in the wind. He takes it in. The breeze and all that dappled sunlight filtered through a mass of green mirrored in the water.

This is everything, he thinks. Communion.

The rocking stops. The water turns opaque like the blackened sky.

"Help!" he hears a voice behind him.

He thinks of Cheryl. Why?

"Dad!" Someone calls. A kid?

"Help!" Louder. Pleading.

Frank scours the boat for a set of oars.

"Dad!"

He knows that voice.

"Help!"

Frank is desperate to call back but can't unclench his jaw, like something's lodged in his esophagus. Pressed against the trachea. Parts of the anatomy he committed to memory when learning CPR. Standard police training.

He uses his bare hands to paddle, to turn the boat around. "Turn! Damnit! Turn!"

The boat holds still, unyielding.

"Dad!"

It's Chris. He's sure of it. What kind of a father wouldn't know the sound of his son's voice!

"Son!" A word recovered.

Frank tries to turn but a searing pain shoots through him.

He blacks out and when he comes around, he's staring up at a white popcorn sky and glassy moon. It's one of those generic ceiling lights, he registers, as a sliver of moonlight bleeds through a misshapen set of steel-grey blinds—exactly the kind that Cheryl detests, preferring those drapes, those goddamn drapes that make him think of funeral homes.

It takes a moment to realize the television's on and he's lying on the sofa, where he must have dozed off, a silver locket clutched in his hand.

25

Kashif tucked away his phone, as if that were all it would take to drown out his dad's voice. "Is there anything to report, then?" he asked Nasser.

Nasser, who had agreed to take the first outdoor shift so Kashif could take his mom home, now did an anxious scan of the lobby. "Nothing so far."

"And did Ishaq-bhai change his mind about private security?"

"You heard the guy! 'Hate and fear can only be vanquished with peace and love!' It's like he's completely out of touch! I mean, where's the shame in protecting people?"

"Do you think he just says that to keep everyone calm?"

"Look, my Uncle Reza and Ishaq-bhai go way back." Nasser put a firm hand on Kashif's shoulder. "He's got a lot to consider, starting with investors who'll get jittery if they think this place is guarded to the hilt, like the Vatican or Fort Knox. If it starts looking like a liability—catch my drift?"

Kashif didn't care for the insinuation that Ishaq-bhai put money before people's lives, and he certainly didn't like second-hand, much less third-hand, reports. But there was no sense trying to dissect Ishaq-bhai's motivations now.

"Trust me," Nasser underscored. "There's no one looking out for us here. No one but *us!*"

"You're right!" Kashif said, trying to forget that he hadn't had the chance to contact Arubah, much less fill his empty stomach.

"And like I reminded the other guys!" Nasser said, catching Kashif's sleeve. "Don't be a hero-number-zero! Signal for back-up first. Then act. Got it?"

"Got it!" Kashif almost lifted up his hand in mock salute, unnerved by the way Nasser treated them like cadets at boot camp. Though, to be fair, he'd been cool about the last-minute change, leaving Kashif the later shift to patrol the Complex grounds.

It was already dark when Kashif stepped out by the emergency exit at the east wing, and he imagined Kamal doing exactly the same thing: taking a walkabout with his flashlight, on the other side of that wall. He zipped up his jacket, noticing flecks of snow lit up by the motion sensor mounted above the exit door. As he stepped into the night he realized it was more than a light snowfall. The area was already blanketed in white.

Making his way round to the back of the building, a set of bright lights and activity attracted his attention. He stiffened and put his hand on his right hip, feeling for an imaginary holster, suddenly alive to the thrill of feeling like a real cop on patrol. As he drew closer to the lights, he heard someone speaking in Urdu. A woman was standing at the loading area by the kitchen, at the back of the Complex, while someone else was tossing several bags of garbage into the city bins.

"Arré, jaldi karro, na!" a woman's voice shouted after a stocky man. They were both dressed to the nines, so the sight of her bossing him to put out the garbage while she stood idly by, complaining about the cold, made Kashif chuckle, though not without a tinge of discomfort over the imaginary weapon he was so eager to draw only seconds earlier.

Things got quiet and dark again as he walked the longest stretch of the building running the length of the swimming pool in the athletic wing. He suppressed a sneeze, and stopped to lift up his collar for some protection from the wind, pausing to take a quick sweep of the area behind him.

The smell of chlorine and the steady whir of a machine assaulted him as he passed the swimming pool filtration pump. He was a few feet from the corner when he heard another sound. It wasn't anything mechanical as far as he could tell—maybe just a raccoon rifling through a plastic bag. When he heard a low whine, almost like a moan, he knew he had to check it out. It was coming from the vicinity of the other emergency exit at the west wing, which he approached as quietly as he could, relieved the snow absorbed the sound of his footsteps.

The moaning became more distinct. He could have sworn it was human, not animal. Had a delivery guy come round this way? But why? This part of the building was closed off.

He inched closer. There was no light under the awning on this side. Maybe the motion sensor was broken, he reasoned. A few feet away from the exit he detected someone silhouetted against the wall. He heard another moan and then a woman's laughter, more like a giggle. He turned on the flashlight he'd been carrying.

"What the fuck!" Two human bodies split apart from an embrace.

"Who's that?" Kashif edged closer.

"None of your business!"

Kashif shone the light on the man.

"Jamshed!" he said, astonished.

He put a spotlight on the woman, who was smoothing down her glittery top. He was right: it *was* Farida. Kamal's sister.

"Get that thing off of us, you idiot!" Jamshed shouted.

"Sorry, I—" Kashif said, his flashlight still locked on their faces.

Jamshed lunged forward clumsily, his hand on his zipper.

"Look, it's off! It's off!" Kashif swore, holding the flashlight up in the air.

"Good! Now scram!" Jamshed turned back to Farida who pulled him under the awning from behind.

"Aren't you supposed to be on watch, like the rest of us?"

"With you losers? Not a chance!"

Kashif was about to warn Jamshed those *losers* included Farida's brother who could just as easily have been the one to walk in on them.

But then he changed his mind, figuring anyone who called himself *Jam* deserved to get caught. He pressed on to the parking lot, the glare from one of the lamp posts blotting out the image of the couple getting it on.

He took a quick survey of the parking lot. Everything was still, the snow muting the lights dotted across the Complex perimeter. He walked down one of the lanes, casually observing how the snow on the cars provided a clue as to how late or early people had arrived, pleased with this little piece of detective work.

As he rounded the next lane, he spotted a few cars from which the snow had been removed, but only in patches, leaving bald spots on the hood or door frame. One of them resembled the Baksh's sedan, so he took a closer look.

Terrorists! A word sprang out in red letters from one of the car doors.

Then, variations on the theme: *Pig-Haters. Extremist Pigs. Muslim Swine.*

He touched the letters. They were tacky and wet, like fresh paint. He sniffed the tip of his fingers. It didn't have the chemical signature of spray paint but it wasn't odorless either. It smelled like . . . blood.

Kashif recoiled, wiping his hands on his coat, his pants—anything to get the red stain off his fingers. He snapped off a few pictures, and hastened to catch up with the other guys, recalling Nasser's warning not to be a "hero-number-zero" and go it alone.

He was a few lanes down when he came across another row of vandalized cars—four windshields bearing the same signature red lettering.

He shone the flashlight over the car to the left, the word *Freedom* appearing vertically below the letter *F.*

The second car bore the letter A. *Against*, he read.

He moved the light over the two cars on the right. The first revealed an I. *Islamic.*

He braced himself for the R on the far right. *Refugees.* It could be worse, he thought, then saw other words peeking through the snow: *Rats. Rapists. Ragheads.*

Kashif's face burned, an unfamiliar sensation welling up inside him. It wasn't fear or anxiety. It was rage. He dabbed at the beads of sweat pooling at his left and right temple, trying to regain his composure. It was only when he stepped back and shone the light over the entire set of cars that he realized the letters weren't arbitrary.

FAIR, he read.

FAIR. He turned the word over, convinced he'd seen those letters somewhere before.

He snapped off another set of pictures before the snow covered the evidence, because that's what it was: evidence—something concrete to show the police when the time came. He texted the pictures to the guys and was about to call them when he thought he felt something or someone move behind him.

He strobed the flashlight over the grounds. For a split second, maybe less, the faintest shadow of a man materialized. Then nothing and a moment of stillness before the figure reappeared under the light cast by a flickering lamp post. He was weaving his way through the parking lot, heading straight for the west wing.

Straight for Jamshed . . . and Farida! Kashif seized up. He dropped the flashlight and started to run, moved by sheer adrenalin and instinct.

Within seconds he was close enough to make out a hooded figure about a head taller than himself. Someone that size should have been able to out-run him, he thought. Something was slowing him down. Then he spotted it—a bag hanging off the guy's shoulder, like a duffle or a gym bag, all his worst fears about a violent attack coming to pass.

"Kashif!" a voice rang through the night, somewhere up ahead.

Kashif couldn't afford to look up, his vision narrowed to the path of pursuit. He was far too close now. Just a few paces apart. He thrust out a hand in the dark and hit on something. The figure hoisted the bag over his shoulder, as if he were trying to shove whatever Kashif had dislodged back into the bag.

Kashif lunged at him this time, his hand latching on and then slipping off an object that felt soft and solid all at once. Almost like cartilage and skin. Like bones made flesh.

The figure stumbled, turned back to look at Kashif. Bouncing flashlights piercing through the snowfall from a distance hit upon a face, and an image on a phone screen flashed across Kashif's peripheral vision.

"Thor?"

More voices. Shouting out a name. Not his.

Kashif stole another look, a faded haircut silhouetted against the strobing lights.

"Chris?"

Confusion in the other's eyes.

"Stop! No! Stop!" Someone was waving down a second figure running directly toward him, oblivious to their cries.

"Jam! Don't!"

A shot, or the echo of a shot, cut through the night, and Kashif felt himself freefall to the ground.

Something dropped but didn't make a sound, the snow, a cushion against the asphalt. A pair of beady eyes on a decapitated head looked on in quiet accusation, a black duffle bag lying open on the ground beside it.

He could have sworn the pig's head was smiling as he mumbled something to the guys standing over him—maybe Ismail, maybe Zafar.

Something about . . . the *Mughal.*

"Call the Mughal," they think he said as Kashif slipped in and out of consciousness.

26

Kauthar brushed back a clump of hair from her son's forehead before dabbing his face with a towel dipped in ice, just as the nurse at the HRH, the Humber River Hospital, had instructed. She tried not to focus on the wide stretch of gauze on his chest. Even without the dressings in view, there was no concealing the drip in his arm, nor the unnerving starts and stops of the heart monitor. Only Kashif's face, with those long lashes curled up at the crease of his peacefully sleeping eyes, was the part of her son she could take in. The rest of this motionless young man . . . well, it was simply not him. How could this be the same boy who doused blueberry jam on parathas and mango pickle on pizzas? The same caring young man who had taken his mother to every one of her medical appointments because *she* was the one who was sick, the one who should have been lying here now, awaiting word from God, that her time had come. Could this really be the child she had raised in a foreign country to which he seemed to belong more than he had ever belonged to her. Was this the baby she had once held in her arms, almost twenty-three years ago, in a hospital room just like this one, with its mint-green walls and sterilized instruments and unsmiling doctors.

Where was *her* Kashif? Where was the child named by a father who fancied his son being a discoverer or pioneer, which Kauthar had dismissed as another one of Hassan's curious ideas. She had acquiesced in favour of the other meaning of the name: Revealer. Explainer. Because she always knew that she would need this child, born to this foreign land, to explain its strangeness to her. She would need him to help her make sense of their life here, and even her place in it. She had not anticipated having to make sense of what such a place could do to him.

Zafar and some of the other boys from the Centre had tried to explain what had happened. About their plan to keep watch on the community after the Rexdale incident at the Masjid Omar Bin Al-Hamad. About their fear that no one was taking the threats against Muslims seriously enough. About the man, or men, Kashif had chased through the parking lot, confirming that Eid night was the target of another hate crime. About how no one had counted on Jamshed, whom she still knew so little about, bringing a gun to the Centre, and his defense that it was dark and the lights across the grounds were few and far between. The snow on the ground had muffled the voices warning him not to fire, he said, insisting that he was out there on his own, even though he knew of the other boys' mission, and that he'd only brought the gun to protect them. When he saw someone being chased, he thought one of them was in trouble. He was just trying to look out for them, because wasn't that what they had wanted in the first place? A lookout team. A first line of defense, not with childish *neighbourhood watches* but with street smarts and someone to fight fire with fire. Till a gun went off. And the wrong man fell while the other escaped.

But the police were not convinced that Kashif was the wrong man. At least that is what it sounded like when they questioned Jamshed.

Even Kauthar had not been spared an interrogation.

Why did your son leave the Islamic Cultural Centre in the middle of the festivities, Mrs Siddiqui? If his goal was to drop you home and return to the Centre, then why did he not ride back with this woman, Bina Baksh? Are you or your son aware Ms Baksh and her family took a recent trip to the Middle East? What is your son's relationship to Ms Baksh?

Kauthar was alone in the room during the police's subsequent visit.

Her heart nearly stopped, convinced that the Angel of Death had come for her son, and she closed her eyes to pray till the drip-drip of the IV gave her another start. Didn't some say the soul left the body like water droplets from a vessel? What if it were the Angel, after all?

She tried to resurrect the prayers buried deep inside her, as if the cancer had not only robbed her body of healthy cells but had also stripped her spirit of those reservoirs of faith.

Oh, Malak al Maut, she began, finally able to retrieve the name for the Angel. She searched for the right Quranic verse for such times and finally settled on the Surah Yasin, which she had last heard at her uncle's funeral. *Surely everything has a heart, and the heart of the Quran is Yasin* . . . She pushed herself to recall the next verse but her mind would not cooperate. She could not—*would not*—remember. Remembering meant acceptance. And how could she accept such a fate for her son.

Kauthar opened her eyes, hoping the Angel would be gone, but two figures remained standing by Kashif's bed. They were both dressed in black, that much she could tell, only this time she heard one of them speaking to Kashif in the slow, methodical way Dr Eleniak always spoke to her, like she was a child or simply hard of hearing.

"How are you feeling, Kashif? Are you able to understand me?"

Kauthar breathed a sigh of relief when she heard her son respond, and instinctively recited the Surah Al-Fatiha, a prayer she knew as intimately as the lines on her palm. *All praises and thanks be to Allah, the Most Beneficent, the Most Merciful. All praises and thanks* . . .

"We would like to ask you a few questions." Kauthar heard a woman's voice and came to Kashif's side, wondering if the doctors were making their rounds. "We understand that you and Jamshed Maker were recently seen at an establishment by the name of Al's Roti Hut. Is that correct?"

The policewoman acknowledged Kauthar's anxious vigil, but pressed on. " . . . And did you and Jamshed Maker have prior dealings? Have you ever received any threats from this man? Were you aware of his past ties to a criminal organization?"

Kashif shook his head more vigorously. "And what is the nature of your association with this group of men—Nasser, Kamal, Omar, . . . Yes, our notes will indicate that you object to them being referred to as a formal group with members."

"Please, my son is very tired," Kauthar managed to get in. "He must rest."

The male officer assured her they wouldn't be much longer, and took over from his partner: "What were you doing out on the grounds of the Islamic Cultural Centre? . . . And what was your intention on the night of," he stopped to look at his notes, "Eid al-Fitr?"

"Eid al-Adha," Kauthar corrected him. "There are two eids."

"Two for the price of one, eh!" the officer chuckled, scratching a line through his notepad. "So, what was your intention on the night of . . . Eid al-Adha."

The moving lines on the heart monitor rose to a peak as Kashif tried to string together more than a few grunts in the affirmative or negative.

"Yes, we are aware of the messages on the cars and of the pigs' heads," the officer continued, unfazed. "We also see you attended a prayer service on the morning of this occasion. Is there some reason you chose to attend *this* service and not one closer to your place of residence?"

The male officer scribbled something in his notebook while the female officer picked up on his line of questioning: "Then, you were present for the sermon delivered by one Sheikh Imam Yusuf Badawi?"

Kashif nodded feebly. Yes.

"Are you aware that Mr Badawi has delivered sermons with radicalized aims, and that he is on a terror watch list?" The officer didn't pause for a response. "Do you share any of Mr Badawi's beliefs?"

No.

"Are you sympathetic to any of the following organizations: ISIS, Al Nusra Front, People's Mujahadeen . . . "

Kashif suppressed a cough, his hand on his chest, and Kauthar buzzed for the nurse. "Please! Enough!"

Hassan Siddiqui rushed into the room with the nurse at his heels. "What's happening? Has Kashif had a setback?"

"Thank you for your cooperation, sir," the male officer said to Kashif, tucking his notebook into a pocket emblazoned with the OPP crest.

"Mr and Mrs Siddiqui," the female officer nodded as they left.

"They upset him too-too much! So many questions!" Kauthar held Kashif's hand as the nurse checked his vitals. Once reassured that he was stable and sedated, Kauthar agreed it was best to step out and take a break.

She and Hassan did a walking tour of the floor, the space between them still tense as live wire. They eventually settled into the waiting room where Hassan found Kauthar a comfortable chair by the window. The room was surprisingly bright and warmed by the morning sun, its penetrating rays hitting the spot where Hassan remained standing. Kauthar studied her husband, his face awash in muddy-grey tones that always signalled he was anxious or unwell. But she had never seen him like this, the blood drained from his cheeks, leaving two dark circles under his eyes, which turned down like question marks, just like his son's.

Hassan muttered something about going to the cafeteria, and offered to get her a cup of tea, but she had to remind him of the peg, of her condition. By now their secrets were out. Hassan knew about her cancer and she knew that things were over with this other woman. At least that's what he said, though she wondered if it even mattered anymore. In the hours that her son's fate was being determined by forces greater than the Indus and the Ravi combined, Kauthar had also resolved to let go of other old attachments, including the shame she bore over Hassan's affair. It was *his* sin, after all. Not hers. All the people who had a hand in their union—their fathers, their families, the maulvi who sanctified their marriage vows, the cousin who helped expedite their visas to Canada—had turned her into that broken doll, with all those pulls and tugs, sometimes this way, sometimes that way. They had rendered her disfigured and mute, even in this new land, which should have placed her outside the paralysing gaze of other people's expectations and doubts.

Seeing Hassan again reminded her that even in his absence it was *his* needs, *his* desires, *his* successes and *his* failings that had consumed her. Like the cancer, he had depleted her, like she was the ghost in a home from which *he* had departed. It was not that she was ready to forgive him; she simply had no more energy to dwell on him—on his betrayal. That would be putting him first all over again, would it not? She had grown up thinking that any man she married would have to come first. Sometimes even over her own children. Or at least that was the order of things in the home she was raised in: first father, then sons, then mother, then daughters. She was the youngest of three daughters and two sons. She was delivered into the world like an afterthought. Maybe this was why her father had marked her out for this life, so far away from home, where her absence seemed to make so little difference to the people and places she would leave behind.

At least Hassan's awareness of her condition had made her feel lighter, stronger, freer. But she wasn't sure if he saw it that way. There was something in his eyes that told her the burden of guilt had shifted from his shoulders to hers, because—how had he put it?—*how could she have let Kashif deal with something as serious as this on his own!*

What was he trying to say—that she was a bad mother? Who was he to judge, when he was the one who had left them to fend for themselves! When she was the one who was wronged so shamelessly! When she *and* Kashif were owed a lifetime of repentance and apology! Then, she recalled those prolonged bouts of illness and disorientation after the chemo, when the world receded and all she could focus on were the excruciating demands of her own body. Those long stretches when she was barely conscious, the chirping of little birds on the balcony, the sensation of a blanket being draped over her shoulders, a door closing or a tap being opened—all of it just part of the derisive noise of a world moving on without her. Had Kashif melded into the background as well? It wasn't as if she hadn't wondered where he was or what he was doing outside his working hours, though she couldn't recall asking where he was going. Was he leaving the house so much because of her? Was he eating well, or was he just surviving on frozen pizzas? She had noticed he no longer kept the television on for long stretches and spent most of his time in his room, his ears plugged into his headphones. Was he trying to stay quiet for her sake? Was he sleeping all right?

"Let me come home." Hassan broke their implicit accord of silence. "When Kashif is discharged, I would like to come home."

Hassan's request should have shocked her, but Tasneem had already primed her for this eventuality, when she had helped fill the hours during Kashif's surgery with her chatter: "Kashif will need his father in the days and weeks ahead, Kauthar-bhain. And you have to think of yourself, too—your own care. You've been through too much on your own, and it's time to let Hassan-bhai take care of you both now. It's time to let him carry the load."

Kauthar could not deny what a relief it would be to have Hassan home again, for everyone's sake, her family in Pakistan still under the impression they were living some fairy tale existence in the West. If Hassan were back, she could stop stalling siblings or relatives from visiting Canada to keep those lies and pretenses intact, and they could simply resume the wholly ordinary routine of their domestic life. But in truth the pretense had begun long before Hassan had walked out of their lives—at least, she had always framed it as *their lives*, a betrayal that extended to Kashif, but she could no longer deny that he had walked out of *her life*. Only her life.

And yet, she was not so foolish as to think of marriage as much more than a stage—didn't their weddings begin on a mandap, under grand arches, a spectacle to behold? Once the pageantry was over, she had never expected her life, behind the scenes, to consist of more than a secondary role as Mrs Hassan Siddiqui, though she had counted on Hassan playing *his* part, too, as a dutiful, faithful husband.

"Excuse me, Mrs Siddiqui?" an unfamiliar voice said.

Kauthar looked up, the hazy outline of a white man the same height and build as those police officers all she could make out through the sun's glare. "The police have come already!" Her defenses kicked in. "Kashif cannot be disturbed now."

"Of course, I can come back another day. I'm just here," the man stopped to clear his throat, "as a friend."

"Oh?" Hassan looked up this time.

The man held out his hand. "My name is Frank. Frank Snyder."

27

Kashif struggled with the remote. His dad was doing the unthinkable, watching local news on the television with him. Eid night had received some attention in the local news but hardly any space on the national level. After days spent in the hospital watching weather forecasts dragged out to feature-length weather stories, or feel-good pieces about recovered pets and good samaritans, Kashif realized why this kind of local reporting had always tried his dad's patience in the past. Now here they were, glued to the local news.

"Would you like some help with that?" Frank offered.

"Can you put it back to the national news for my dad?"

"Of course." Frank surfed the channels till he settled on a twenty-four-hour news network. "Is there anything else I can get you? Some water?"

"Maybe another cup of crushed ice. Dad went to get me some Gatorade, but it might be a while." Kashif peered out into the hall, wondering if his mom had finally gone home to get some rest. She wouldn't have left for a minute had his dad not been with him, and it felt good to see that at least some of the tension between his parents had abated. It had been more palpable than the hole in his side, at least in the first few days in the hospital.

Frank had caught wind of the shooting, he'd explained, and remembered what Kashif had said about the letter with the clear threat, and their special Muslim religious day—"as big as Christmas." Something made him suspect the worst and he called the Sixth Division for a full report, and learned that a young guy by the name of Kashif Siddiqui had been taken to the Humber River Hospital.

"It must be good to have your dad here," Frank said.

"Yeah." Kashif exhaled. He didn't know where things would go from here, but he'd be lying if he said it didn't feel right to have his dad close at hand again.

"Is all forgiven?"

Kashif glanced at the television, a woman with big teeth announcing that most of southern Ontario was still under a severe winter storm advisory.

"Dad seems to think so," Kashif said, as the news anchor resumed her summary of the day's events. "But I don't know what Mom's thinking. She never even told Dad about the cancer. Can you believe it!"

"Sure, I guess I can. I mean, people deal with illness in different ways—"

"It doesn't excuse what he's done, but . . . " Kashif put his hand to his chest, clearly in some distress.

"Maybe we should talk about this later," Frank said, pouring out a glass of water.

Kashif took a sip and lay back. "What about you and your son, Chris? Have you seen him yet?"

"He's still keeping his distance." Frank squinted, blinded by the strips of light streaming through the set of warped hospital blinds, wondering if this was why Cheryl couldn't stand them. "I can't tell you more than that . . . for now."

"You were discussing an arrest with my dad?"

"Yes, the police have tracked down the founder of this group, FAIR."

"FAIR." Kashif recalled the word sprayed on the cars in the parking lot, each snow-tinged letter unleashing an avalanche of . . . it seemed too easy to call it hatred. Hatred was fire, not ice. Hatred seethed, unseen, in lumps of coal and volcanic magma as much as it raged out in the open, consuming homes and forests with brute ferocity.

"I saw it out there, you know. FAIR, chiseled into the wall of the little mosque. I guess I'm not worth much as a cop anymore, or I would have followed up on it, eh?"

"Nobody made the connection! Not even the cops on duty!" Kashif struggled to sit up. "But there's something else. Something I need to tell you about . . . the night of the attack."

"Oh?"

"For a second, and I mean just for a second, I thought I recognized the guy out there—on Eid night." Kashif decided to just come out and say it: "I thought I saw your son."

"Chris! What do you mean? How would you even recognize him?"

"That day in the coffee shop, when you tried to call him . . . I saw his picture on the phone screen."

"Look, these things happen in the blink of an eye." Frank retrieved his phone and rubbed his thumb over it like he was holding something back. He had made a few inquiries about the suspect linked to FAIR. As far as he knew, they hadn't established that he was the one at the Islamic Cultural Centre—not yet, anyway.

"I'm sorry, you must hate me for thinking it was him, but I swear I didn't tell anyone, not even Dad! In fact, I've been so out of it, I can't say what part of that night was real and what part I dreamed up!" Kashif reached for the cup of crushed ice, comforted by the shock of cold against his skin. "All the same, I thought I should tell you . . . I mean, I thought you should know. But now it looks like it doesn't matter. It looks like they found the guy."

"Yeah . . . it looks like it," Frank said vaguely. "Hey, is that why . . . is that why you took the bullet? Because you thought the guy out there was my son?"

"I don't know, it all happened so fast . . . I didn't know what I was doing."

"Maybe so . . . " Frank pushed his finger through the warped slats at the window and peered outside.

Kashif imagined the snow covering the parking lot, just as it had done that night, a night he had in his mind on instant replay. Now, with news of an arrest, he wondered why he hadn't been asked to ID the suspect. But the more he thought about it, the less certain he felt about what he had or hadn't seen, so what would he say? What *could* he say except the guy he had chased that night was tall. He wore a hoodie. He had a bag slung over his shoulder. He dropped it and for a second, maybe less, he saw a face. Or the outline of a face. For the briefest moment it looked familiar. Or maybe it was just the trick of the light. That faded haircut. Then he heard a shot. He didn't have time to think. He just reacted and pushed the guy out of the way. Then he saw the strangest thing: a decapitated head—a pig's head lying on the ground beside him. One of several, the police had confirmed, found in that duffle bag along with a jar of pig's blood. Apparently, the guy had planned to erect the decapitated heads around the Centre. Then everything went dark.

But for some reason—maybe the part of him that felt like a cop withholding a key piece of evidence—he had needed to tell Frank about what he saw that night. However ridiculous it sounded, however much it jeopardized this odd connection they seemed to have made. Maybe he was hoping Frank could clear things up. Maybe he just needed to say it out loud and get it off his chest. He bit down on an ice cube and took a pained breath. "Some cop *I'd* make, right!"

Frank remained planted by the window. "Oh, I wouldn't say that, Kashif."

Kashif stirred on hearing Frank pronounce his name right for once.

"What you boys did was pretty foolhardy, there's no doubt about it," Frank continued. "But if you're wondering how this will affect your future in the police force, I'd say you've got nothing to worry about. So long as you commit to some physiotherapy and getting your body good and strong again."

Kashif touched his bandaged chest. He wondered if he should tell Frank what had been on his mind since the shooting. That he was having a change of heart about applying to the police academy. That he was no longer certain about becoming a cop. He hesitated to say it out loud because he knew he'd be asked for an explanation and, at least for now, he had none to offer. His thoughts were crystal particles again, a dance of fractals. With one turn, they were coloured by the way the police had interrogated him after the shooting. And it wasn't just the nature of the questions; there was something about the way they looked at him. He was loath to admit it, but it was the same way Frank had looked at those boys in the coffee shop. And with another turn, he questioned his own impulses on Eid night. What had he hoped to achieve chasing after a guy who could have been armed? And what if *he* had carried a gun? Would he have had the same instinct as Jamshed: to shoot first, ask questions later? Even if they had security that night—even if they had the full force of the law behind them—would this have really changed the outcome? And yet, with another turn, he could see the value of having the law on his side. On *being* the law. And he wouldn't waste time establishing the obvious: *They* weren't the enemy! They were trying to protect themselves. They were just trying to celebrate a holy day, without fear. Without incident.

Kashif circled back to Ishaq-bhai's comments to the reporter outside the little mosque—his invitation for open dialogue had seemed like such a cop-out. Kashif had felt so let down, betrayed, like Ishaq-bhai was just handing over all his power to a criminal. Like he was proposing to hold a conference among equals. But now he wondered if Ishaq-bhai wasn't wrong to think it was time to have such conversations—to open the door just enough to adjust the terms of engagement. But even so, it took two parties to engage, and Ishaq-bhai's invitation for open dialogue had fallen on deaf ears.

Kashif could only conclude that there had to be another way. A path not yet taken.

Frank glanced at the group of people collecting in the hall. "Well, it looks like you've got quite the fan club out there, so I should really get going—"

"Please stay. There's something else. About the police."

28

"Aruba, Jamaica, ooh, I wanna take you . . . " Marisol sang into Arubah's ear.

"Urgh! Not that song!"

"I thought that would get your attention! Where did you disappear, anyway?"

"Oh, nowhere! I was just thinking about your parents. How will they know which room Kashif is in? I don't think they even know his last name!"

"They're enterprising. They'll manage."

"Excuse me," Arubah tried to get the nurse's attention again.

"I'll be right with you," a buttoned-up voice was barely audible behind a raised ledge.

Arubah hadn't planned on coming to the hospital with Marisol—not after everything her friend had been through, but she didn't count on finding *herself* triggered by it all. She hadn't set foot in a hospital since she was that little girl watching her mom fall to her knees when the doctor came out of the operating room. Now this was the second hospital visit in a single week involving someone she cared about.

"Kashif Siddiqui's room number?" Marisol stuck her face over the desk.

The nurse swivelled her chair to retrieve a chart. "Room 86. Down the hall to your left."

"Nice work!" Arubah was relieved to see some of Marisol's spunkiness return. "And, in case I didn't say it already, you're awesome for coming with me today."

"To be honest, I think we all need to focus on something else," Marisol said. "And you know my folks aren't the type to sit around. They want to be useful in the case against—you know."

Arubah feather-touched the sling on her friend's arm. It was a reminder of the assault—a reminder of how breakable they all were. But it was also a testament to Marisol's strength. If she hadn't fought off that guy, Arubah could only imagine what else she might have had to endure, her mind always straying back to the cases they read about in Professor March's course. In fact, Marisol had put up such a fight that her assailant used the gash on his face to claim that *he* was the victim. At least the cops weren't buying his story but they couldn't be sure what the outcome of a trial would be—whether it would reduce the sentence from sexual assault to some lesser charge.

Marisol cradled her sling with her good arm as they looked for Room 86. "Then again, I think they feel so helpless right now, so Mom's channelling her energies wherever she can. Really, she's been on a bit of a crusade in Quebec since Dad's friend was racially pro-filed, remember?"

"How can I forget? Did those poor people ever file a human rights case, then?"

"Mom says half the battle is convincing people to lodge a formal complaint. All it takes is that one person . . . So far only Bassam's agreed to do it. The others backed out."

Marisol's voice trailed off and Arubah didn't have to imagine where it had gone. She would have to be that "one person" now, testifying against Alex Petrossian.

"She says new laws are rarely created unless there's a long trail of evidence to warrant them." Marisol ran a hand along the metal rail-ing mounted to the wall till her face contorted, like she had received an electric shock. "I guess that's partly why she's curious to hear more about your friend—I mean, your *boyfriend's*—story."

"He's not my boyfriend!" Arubah protested.

"I stand corrected: your *future* boyfriend!" Marisol winked.

"If you say so!" Arubah blushed. Seeing Marisol lighten up and even tease her a little was worth the price of admission.

"Here it is!" Arubah mentally prepared herself. "Room 7-86." She had been desperate to see Kashif the minute they heard about the shooting, but she had held back, wanting to give Marisol all of her support.

"My goodness, it took forever to get parking!" Arubah could hear Isabel all the way down the hall. "And then Amin heard you say the *seventeenth* floor, not the *seventh*!"

"What did I tell you!" Marisol said, but Arubah's attention was taken up by two men and a familiar-looking guy coming out of Kashif's room. They were talking in hushed tones, though Arubah noticed one man—a white man—had stayed behind with Kashif.

"Achha, sunno, Ishaq-bhai!" Arubah heard one of the men, his body angled away from the new visitors. "Please stay for a few minutes. I'd like to have a word."

"Of course, Hassan-bhai."

Hassan-bhai? As in Kashif's dad! Arubah gasped. He was here! Where else would he be, she rationalized. The similarity between father and son, so obvious now, blurred the sharper edges of that image of Hassan arm-in-arm with another woman, as she'd seen him before.

"Ishaq-bhai, I'm still not clear why things got so out of control," Hassan said, even his voice an accented version of Kashif's. "I've got my son's side of the story, but I'd like to hear yours. Were you aware there was a threat against the Centre that night?"

The chatter ceased, all eyes on Ishaq-bhai.

"No one could have known anything for certain," Ishaq-bhai replied.

"But what about that letter? Kashif and his friends were convinced there was a threat."

"I'm not sure how the boys could have known that." Ishaq-bhai threw Zafar a mildly admonishing look.

"So, you knew there was a threat?" Hassan persisted.

"Sadly, communities like ours receive idle threats all the time. The police determined there was little to be done at the time, and on this we were all in agreement: there was no cause for alarm."

"And yet here's my son lying in a hospital bed with a bullet in him!" Hassan rubbed his hands across his face.

"It's not much of a consolation, I know, but Jamshed Maker has confessed to the shooting, and possession of a stolen firearm. He will be tried for it."

"But you know I'm not just talking about that! Jamshed may have pulled the trigger, but there was a whole series of events leading up to that moment. Like why those boys felt they had to be out there to begin with!"

Ishaq-bhai put a gentle hand on Hassan's shoulder. "Hassan-bhai, if there was any way this senseless tragedy could have been prevented, I assure you—"

"But that's just it, Ishaq!" Hassan protested, the fact that he had dropped the brotherly term of endearment not lost on Arubah. "It *could* have been prevented! If only it was taken more seriously from the start, it could have been prevented!"

Ishaq-bhai put his hands together. "Now that the police have apprehended a suspect, we will get some answers about Eid night and, inshallah, the earlier attack on the mosque. But we must be patient and let those who are trained to protect our cities do their jobs. And we can best protect ourselves by living our lives—by honouring our way of life." Ishaq-bhai parted his hands and raised them up. "The rest is up to Allah, the Merciful."

"But what about this supremacist group? I heard there's a connection between FAIR and this recent spate of hate crimes," Isabel stepped in.

"The police are looking into that as well, ma'am."

"Arresting one person here or there won't be enough to shut them down," Hassan countered.

Isabel edged in towards Ishaq-bhai till they were face to face. "He's right, you know! Only more weeds grow in stagnant ponds."

Arubah could see from Isabel's pinched brow that there was a lot more she wished to say but Amin clutched her hand: "We can appreciate the impossible position you're in, sir," he said graciously to Ishaq-bhai, then turned to Marisol, "as we can all appreciate the depth of our pain when we see our children come to harm."

"Alhamdulillah," Ishaq-bhai replied with a courteous bow. He turned to Hassan who was still keeping one eye on Kashif: "Hassan-bhai, I'll check in on Kashif again tomorrow, if that is all right with you." Without waiting for a response, he added, "And please give Kashif's dearest mother my salaams."

Hassan seemed to stop himself short of pursuing Ishaq-bhai down the hall. "I'm sorry. Forgive my manners." He turned to Arubah and the Martinez-Hamids. "I'm Hassan Siddiqui—Kashif's father. I presume you're all here to see my son?"

"Dad!" Kashif's cry was loud enough to send Hassan charging back into the room.

"What's happened? Shall I call the doctor?"

"No, Dad! It's not me! Something's happened! Something bad!"

Arubah couldn't help herself and gently knocked on the door. "Is everything OK?" She was close enough to see Kashif pointing to the words "Breaking News" scrolling across the television screen.

A news anchor appeared with a grave expression: *"We are coming to you live from Quebec City where there has been a deadly shooting. Police are reporting three dead . . . "*

"Arubah!" Kashif said, a little winded. "Please come in! Everyone, come!"

"Police are confirming this was a targeted attack. The mosque was open to congregants attending its special Friday prayer service . . . " the anchor continued.

Arubah ushered Marisol and her parents into the room, trapping Frank in the corner by the window. The anchor reappeared and repeated the few details she had already provided and everyone fell silent, a collective gasp triggered by a ringing phone. It had a retro ring that Kashif instantly recognized as his dad's.

"Hello? . . . " Hassan tried to keep his voice down before passing the phone to Kashif.

"Yes, I'm all good, Mom," Kashif reassured his mom as he gestured for someone to turn up the volume.

"*We now have word that Monsieur Guy Durocher, the police commissioner of the Sûreté du Québec, will be providing a briefing in the next hour,*" the anchor was saying. "*In the meantime, we can confirm that one young white male in his late twenties entered the mosque in a neighbourhood just south of Quebec's historic city centre.*"

"Why don't they tell us something about the shooter!" Hassan impugned. "What if he's connected to—"

"FAIR," Frank completed his thought.

Kashif said a quick goodbye to his mom, hoping she wasn't watching the news at home. On the one hand, she was a different person, speaking to the doctors and his dad with a confidence he'd never seen before. On the other hand, she was *classic mom*, blaming herself for what happened on Eid night, telling Tasneem Aunty that if she had only asked him to stay home with her, none of this would have happened.

"*Approximately sixty practitioners are reported to have been in attendance at this service,*" the anchor continued. "*The as-yet unidentified shooter was wearing a ski mask when he entered the mosque and opened fire. Witnesses say the gun was emptied and left at the scene.*"

Arubah found herself quietly reciting the Surah al-Kauthar—"In the name of Allah, we have given you al-Kauthar, a river in paradise." It was the only prayer that came to mind as she hoped against hope that there were no more casualties to report. No more deaths.

"*Our local correspondent confirms the suspect has been apprehended.*" The anchor's voice bore the urgency of the latest update. "*We repeat: the suspect has been apprehended a few metres from the Pont du Québec—the Quebec Bridge—across the lower Saint Lawrence . . .* "

"They'll just say it's some crackpot acting alone!" Zafar interjected, confirming where Arubah had seen him before: with the group of guys Kashif was speaking to on Eid night.

"The police are now also reporting eighteen people have been killed. Sixteen adult males, and two minors under the age of thirteen. Another dozen or so people have been rushed to hospital with a range of minor to life-threatening injuries."

"Por dios!" Isabel put her hand on her mouth.

"Jesus Christ, this *is* bad—real bad!" Frank remarked from the corner where he seemed to have settled in for the long haul.

"Call it what it is, damnit!" Marisol shouted at the TV. "It's a terrorist attack! He's a terrorist!"

Amin grabbed his daughter's hand.

The anchor repeated the headlines, promising live updates as more information poured in, and everyone broke out into hushed exchanges, desperate to process the horror unfolding in real-time, right before their eyes.

They waited for more news. Together.

Epilogue

"Sometimes she's been as wide as the mighty Nile, and other times as thin as an undertaker's smile," Frank sang, his paddle beating on the water like a hand on a drum.

"I don't know how you can sing and row at the same time!" Kashif called out from the other canoe that he and Arubah were struggling to keep from tipping over.

"Well, I've got quite the co-pilot with me, here!" Frank winked at Marisol.

Frank was right. Marisol had spent enough summers by Quebec's lakes and rivers to know how to paddle a canoe, but it had been a while since she had been on the water. She had jumped at the chance to join Arubah and Kashif on their afternoon excursion to Frank's neck of the woods west of Toronto, where he had settled into a new home close to his beloved Grand River.

Frank didn't have the heart to return to police life. Besides, the OPP had moved on without him and he no longer felt he belonged there. Or maybe it was the mass murder in Quebec and the events that followed that had shaken him up in ways he hadn't counted on. Seeing how the perpetrator was not much older than Chris. Seeing his parents defending him to the bitter end, though he had confessed to everything, including his involvement with ultra-nationalists operating out of France and Quebec. And then the other incident—the hate crimes closer to home—that had almost cost Kashif his life. The founder of the group, FAIR, had made no bones about his supremacist views, but he had vehemently denied being at the Islamic Cultural Centre on Eid night, and so it was still uncertain whom Kashif had chased out there in the parking lot. The one arrest had enabled the police to shut down the FAIR network, terminate all of its social media accounts and effectively stamp out its virtual footprint, but Frank couldn't shake Marisol's mother's words, that "only more weeds grow in stagnant ponds." And then there was Chris. As far as his son was concerned, not too much had changed. He was still holed up in that basement, glued to those headphones. He was still unable to hold down a job for any length of time. Frank had even confronted him about his whereabouts on Eid night—what kind of a cop would he be if he didn't? But that had only widened the gulf between them, and Cheryl had closed ranks too, as if *he* were the enemy now! And yet . . . Frank remained hopeful—hopeful enough to start calling the Big-C, the Big Change. He was done with the cancer. He was ready for the life to come. And when his son was ready to come up for air he'd be here. Here, in the one place that wouldn't pull them both under. He would make sure of it. He *wasn't* his old man.

"Hey, you lovebirds are falling behind!" Marisol yelled, thrilled to be spending time with Arubah before she had to take off again. So far, she had been unable to find her way back to university, despite Professor Greenwood's encouragement to pursue graduate studies under his supervision. She had wanted to put as much distance between herself and the dorm, the campus, the city—anything that reminded her of Eid night. But when Alex Petrossian was convicted of the lesser charge of physical assault, she found herself holding court in her own mind, night after night. Only, she was the one on trial, condemned to feel she hadn't done enough, said enough—the scars on her body not evidence enough of his intentions. When her mom said she'd be working on another reparations case in Guatemala, she needed little convincing that it was time to accompany her, and she imagined herself heading south like the monarch butterflies. Only this time she would not just be the gringa from the North. They were even planning a special mother-daughter trip out to the springs of Nacimiento. It seemed like a good place to start.

"There's a good clearing up ahead!" Frank brought his paddle in and rested it on his lap, waiting patiently for Kashif and Arubah to catch up. "And rumour has it Arubah's mom has packed us a big lunch!"

"Actually, my dad made it!" Kashif said.

After a few 360-degree turns in the water, and some instructions yelled over by Marisol to keep them from capsizing, Arubah and Kashif managed to steer their way towards the embankment, panting as they clambered out of the canoe.

"Hey, there are those willow roots Frank was talking about!" Arubah peered down at the crimson rhizomes hugging the riverbank.

"It really does look like red licorice!" Marisol stretched out beside her.

"They look more like veins to me. Like those little capillaries we learned about in the anatomy section in Psych class," Arubah said.

"Time to eat," Kashif said, fishing out a fragrant picnic of kebabs wrapped in naan.

"These are amazing!" Marisol dabbed a drizzle of coriander chutney from the side of her mouth.

"Yeah, who knew Dad could cook. Mom was always the cook—"

"I'm sorry, Kashif," Marisol sighed.

"Kauthar-Aunty would have liked it here," Arubah broke the pall of sadness taking over the group. Kauthar's cancer had gone into remission, giving them hope, only to have it return with a vengeance. "There are so many birds."

Kauthar's death had left them with another shared wound, Arubah thought. Another axis of connection. She had feared the loss would weaken Kashif's resolve to find a way forward, especially since he'd given up on applying to the police academy, but the shock of those events—Eid night, the Quebec massacre, losing Kauthar—seemed to have had the opposite effect. Like a flash flood, the destruction was as swift as it was upbraiding, leaving them disoriented and grieving, but also pushing them past limits that had once seemed impossible to surmount. And now here she was, plunging headfirst into other uncharted waters, heading to law school the same year Kashif was starting a child and youth studies program at a local college. He wasn't sure where that would lead, but with his experience as a big brother at the Centre, he finally felt he was on the right track. She wondered how this might change things for them, each one setting off on new paths that would consume so much of their time and energy. Though she was secure in the knowledge that the path which had brought them together was like the point where two rivers meet—as irreversible as the forces that ensured their confluence.

"Whoa! That's spicy!" Frank grunted, reaching for his water flask, making them all laugh.

Eventually they settled back, their bellies full, and the sound of the water gently lapping against the rocks lulled them into a quiet repose.

"Hey, are you singing again, Frank?" Marisol asked, her face shaded by her baseball cap.

A chorus of voices filtered through the trees.

"That could be Brittany and Joey!" Frank sprang up. "My niece and her husband! I had invited them to join us but they said they were involved in some kind of river-walking-thing this weekend!"

"You mean a water walk?" Marisol said.

"That's it!" Frank said. "It's a big march along the Grand River, from source to mouth. To raise awareness about pollution, they said. Like an environmental protest, I guess you could call it."

"Didn't you write about something like that for one of your classes?" Arubah asked Marisol.

"Kind of! It was based on one of Greenwood's lectures. He said the water walkers walk the entire watershed, giving thanks to the water and praying for its protection. It's an Indigenous-led ceremony but it's open to everyone." Marisol clambered up a boulder, trying to catch sight of the water walkers through a dense tangle of vegetation. "I remember him saying that it shouldn't be seen as a protest march—that it's a sacred journey, not a political one."

"It sounds like they're making their own path through the forest since not all the trails reach the banks," Frank said, as the voices grew fainter. "But we may just meet up with them at another point down river."

"Should we get back on the water, then?" Kashif asked, stretching his arms and legs.

"Yeah, but I think we should shake things up a bit this time!" Marisol proposed. "Me and Kashif, Arubah and Frank!"

Kashif held out a hand to Arubah and then gathered up the food containers, reserving a piece of naan someone had nibbled on. The way he methodically broke off little pieces, scattering them on the rocks, made Arubah recall her visits with Kauthar in the months before she died. Kashif was always so annoyed by the birds collecting on their balcony, but now he was the one who couldn't let a plate of crumbs or an uneaten pizza crust go to waste.

Kashif turned over the last of the open food containers, shaking out whatever remained, before helping get the canoes back on the water. It felt good to be out of the city. The city was where his mom lay buried, in a multifaith cemetery, but for some reason he could feel her presence more strongly out here by the water. He was beginning to see the force of will and courage it must have taken to come here—that made all kinds of people like his parents leave behind everything and everyone they knew to start all over again. Yet, there was no one to greet his mom on arrival. There was no Arabian Sea waiting at the base of the Indus with open arms. But she was part of this land now, deep in the earth, under the same layers of sediment he imagined moving below them, reshaping the path of the river.

Acknowledgements

I am especially grateful to Nurjehan Aziz, for seeing something of value in this work, and for giving such voices and stories a safe and unfettered platform. Finding one's work under the editorship of M G Vassanji is a boon to any writer's credentials, and this book is so much the better for his perspicacious editorial eye. Thanks also to Marketing Assistant, Crystal Shi, for taking such good care of me and my book at all stages. The book has found a truly welcoming home at Mawenzi.

I was fortunate to have such esteemed early readers as Myriam J A Chancy and Claire Tacon. A special thanks to Royal Society of Canada fellow, David T McNab, for providing his expertise on Indigenous land and treaty rights, and on the history of Waterloo, Ontario. Freelance book editor Aeman Ansari provided, with generosity and enthusiasm, not one but several rounds of invaluable feedback, at a time when the story felt adrift and rudderless—for this, I shall always be grateful. Others, whose support came at a time when I needed their encouraging words and endorsements the most, include Kamal Al-Solaylee, Farzana Doctor, Carrianne Leung, Ute Lischke, Soraya Peerbaye, Priti Sharma-Devata, Sanchari Sur, Kathryn Wardropper, Jenny Heijun Wills and Rahul Varma. I am always buoyed by the support of my colleagues and friends at Wilfrid Laurier University (Jenny Kerber, Carol Duncan, Katherine Spring, Jing Jing Chang, Eleanor Ty, Tamas Dobozy, to name a few . . .). As poet-scholar-confidante Tanis MacDonald has taught me, writing may be a solitary activity, but community is everything.

No undertaking is ever complete without at least a million WhatsApp exchanges with my darling siblings, Nooreen Pirbhai and Reza Pirbhai—thank you both for your patient ear, your solidarity and love. (And thanks to my dearest nephew, Ilyas Pirbhai, for helping his auntie navigate video game culture!)

And to Ronaldo Garcia, who takes every step of the writing journey with me—for better or worse, these stories are as much yours as they are mine. Always.

Mariam Pirbhai is the author of the short story collection *Outside People and Other Stories*, winner of the 2018 IPPY Gold Medal for Multicultural Fiction and the 2019 American BookFest Award for the Short Story. It also ranked among CBC's top ten "must read" books of 2017. *Isolated Incident* is her first novel. The daughter of Pakistani immigrants, Pirbhai is Professor of English at Wilfrid Laurier University, where she teaches and specializes in postcolonial studies and creative writing.